LOCKDOWN PHANTOM #3

Compiled & Edited by

D. Kershaw | Maggie Pawsey | S.N. Graves

Also available and coming soon from Black Hare Press

DARK DRABBLES ANTHOLOGIES

WORLDS
ANGELS
MONSTERS
BEYOND
UNRAVEL

APOCALYPSE
LOVE
HATE
OCEANS
ANCIENTS

BHP WRITERS' GROUP SPECIAL EDITIONS

STORMING AREA 51
EERIE CHRISTMAS
BAD ROMANCE
TWENTY TWENTY

OTHER VOLUMES
DEEP SPACE
WHAT IF?
KEY TO THE KINGDOM
DEEP SEA
BEYOND THE REALM

Twitter: @BlackHarePress
Facebook: BlackHarePress
Website: www.BlackHarePress.com

Cover DesignDawn Burdettwww.dmburdett.com
FormattingBen Thomas www.blackharepress.com

Editing D. Kershaw www.blackharepress.com
Maggie Pawsey
S.N. Graveswww.sngraves.com

Read TeamDavid Greendavidgreenwritercom.wordpress.com
Jennifer Hatfieldjhatfieldauthor.wixsite.com/website
Jodi Jensenjodijensenwrites.wordpress.com
Lyndsay Ellis-Hollowayauthorlyndseyellisholloway.webador.co.uk
Stacey Jaine McIntoshwww.staceyjainemcintosh.com

TABLE OF CONTENTS

OEO

By Hari Navarro

I hadn't visited it for many years. It's like anything I suppose; the more time rolls forward, the more things get left behind. But this place was special, and I should never have left it alone for as long as I did.

My grandfather was a fisherman. Not one who owned or worked on a boat. Not one of those souls who sliced out into the surf and felt at perfect ease as the land fell away far beneath. I think he would have loved that though, to live upon the waves.

I know he would.

But as with them, salt and sand lived in his hair and in the deep cracks of his skin, and so he was no less hardy as he waded out and into the swell. Fearless, no matter how rough it was, he'd push through up to his knees and sometimes up to his waist and then he'd do it. That awesome thing where he whipped with all his might the great rod that he gripped in the iron clench of his fists. Forever searching for those great snapping beasts that shone as they were pulled through the light and up and onto the shore.

As with all lovers of the catch, my grandfather had a favoured and secret spot where he would go and hide from my grandmother and look for not only fish but also man-made things that washed up amongst the drifting wood. He loved it here. This remote tiny cove, this bay far too small for even a name, upon which now I stand. And, again, the wind whips the foam from the waves and drives its salt sting to my face.

I missed that. I missed its taste.

My grandfather has been dead for many years now, and so I guess it's OK to tell you about Oeo. It's not a town, just farmland, and I think there was a pub but, maybe, now there is not.

Oeo.

My grandfather would joke relentlessly that it is the same forward as it is backward. Not so much a joke as it was a statement of fact. But, then, he was that special flavour of man that could find a smile in anything. Even the horrors of war.

We had family friends that owned a dairy farm in Oeo, and my grandfather would drive me in his beloved blue station wagon through the hoof worn muddy rut of its fields. He was a fucking maniac. Hardened by war and a youth of devil-may-care, he'd pummel that old wreck at breakneck speed only to swerve and slide to a halt but mere feet from where the cliff-top slumped and fell away into the chomp of the Tasman Sea's relentless, gnawing bite.

Then, with his backpack filled with the stench of bait that permeated the sandwiches my grandmother had made, and his heavy rods hoisted atop his shoulder, he'd disappear down the sheer face of the cliff. A makeshift ladder made of driftwood and stolen street signs led us down to this secret spot. A ladder that could only be found if you knew exactly where to look, the secret passage to the parapet outcrop of boulders from atop which we'd sit and wait for as long as it took to feel the tug of the fish.

I stand here now with Ethan, my youngest son. His hand blue in mine, and I look and I see my grandfather. I see Frank up there on the rocks. He is not someone else, nor a trick of the light, though I have to squint through the lash of the rain.

It is him.

In this moment, I know. I know that if allowed to, memories can curdle and rot. But that the most precious moments don't fade in time; they linger and they wait.

His skin is grey and paper-thin and riddled with holes, and his ruined shirt flaps as the salt and wind seep through and crash and beat in the hollow of his chest.

"What are you waiting for, old man?" I shout out into the wind, and the tiny blue hand that wasn't even born when the old man died tightens.

Frank turns and he smiles. Fuck, I love this old bugger.

"It's the same way backward as it is forward!" he replies, and I know he's not talking about Oeo.

And the words that carry on the icy gusts warm me and the tip of his rod suddenly cranes and points out into the swell.

"You see him, right?" I say to the wide-eyed boy at my side.

"Yes, Dad, I most surely can, and I think that he's got a fish."

First published on 365tomorrow.com, 2019

THE BECKONING

By Frederick Pangbourne

"Louis, did you really think I would never find out?" The voice on the other end of the phone asked.

Louis sat up straight on the couch and

set his rock glass of iced vodka down on the coaster that rested on a glass coffee table. It was a most peculiar way to open a conversation when calling another. There had been no informal introduction as a simple 'Hello' or 'May I speak to Louis?' No, the male voice that called him was being direct and to the point.

"Who's speaking?" Louis inquired.

"Now, Louis, we're not really going to play games, are we? You know damn well who this is." The voice retained its casual tone.

"Styles?"

"See. You knew who it was, and why shouldn't you? You've been sleeping with my wife for the last couple of months."

Louis leaned forward and grabbed the

glass from the table and polished it off in one swig. "What can I do for you, Styles?" He attempted to strengthen his voice with authority, but it sounded anything but that.

"I just wanted to let you know that I now know. That's all." Style's voice was still relaxed and in control.

"And?"

"And nothing. Just that I applaud the two of you for being able to keep your secret sexual encounters so discrete from me all this time."

"You treat her like shit, Styles. What did you think would happen?"

Styles chuckled on the other end of the receiver. "Some would suggest otherwise, Louis, but that is not the only reason I am calling you tonight. No. You see, I have a proposition for you."

"A proposition?" Louis was now standing and pacing the length of his living room.

"Yes, a proposition. Just to show you that there are no hard feelings. Now that the fact that my wife is an adulteress has been brought into light, I am willing to give her up. To you, of course, if you are still willing to take her?"

"I don't understand."

"Simply put, I am handing her over to you without any legal actions or hired thugs to break your legs being involved. No. I will hand her over to you and all you have to do is meet her in the allotted time given."

"Stop playing games, Styles! All that talking in riddles impresses no one. What have you done to Cyndi?" His voice finally discovered the strength and fortitude it lacked earlier.

"You mean like the games the two of you played behind my back for so long? My deal is plain and simple, Louis. I have a large cottage in the country about an hour and a half from you. Inside the cottage, Cynthia is awaiting you. You need to get there and listen to what she has to say within the given time, and I'll wipe my hands of the both of you. Plain and simple."

"Bullshit! Here you go with your games again…and what do you mean listen to what she has to say? What did you do, Styles? You better not have done anything to her." Louis had moved to another room in his apartment and was now pacing in the kitchen.

"Shut up, Louis, and take down this address. 704 Maple Avenue. It's to the cottage. It is now 8:47pm. You have until 11:30 to be there and to your concerned question, she's fine. You just get your sorry ass up there by then or all bets are off. I'll call you then." The phone clicked as Styles hung up on his end.

Louis pulled his cell phone from his ear and looked at the words 'unknown caller' on the screen. That son-of-a-bitch got the last word in on that one.

Louis stared at the phone until the screen went black and set it aside. He had met Styles and Cyndi about six months ago at a charity dinner. Something involving wounded veterans, he believed. It seemed like a lifetime ago now that he thought back to that night. The three of them had sat at the same table. Styles a successful entrepreneur at fifty-eight, who rose to his current status of wealth and power through profitable real estate investments. Cyndi was twenty years his junior and the ideal trophy wife. The only problem, as Louis had stated on the phone, was he treated her like shit. Styles was the type of man who needed to be waited on constantly and was quick with his sharp tongue when it came to him lashing out insults and belittlements when his needs were not pampered.

Louis moved into his bedroom and changed from basketball shorts and a tank top into a faded pair of jeans and a grey sweatshirt. He wasn't sure what type of game Styles was up to, but he would play into it. Especially if Cyndi was being subjected to this inexplicable scheme of his. Grabbing the keys to his Lexus, he was out the door exactly thirteen minutes after Styles had hung up.

He was making more than an efficient time on his drive up to the cottage. Being a Tuesday night, there was minimal traffic leaving the city and taking the parkway north, far from the densely populated areas to the more deficiently inhabited regions of the state. He guessed that at his current pace, he would arrive at Styles' country home with fifteen minutes to spare.

As he pulled off the exit, leaving the parkway behind, his mind drifted back again to the first night he had met Cyndi.

They had met at the bar while she was getting Styles his usual scotch and soda. Louis was an editor at a popular magazine based in the city and attending charity events such as that one that night usually drew his presence. He recalled her black, one shoulder cocktail dress. The way her long blonde hair stretched passed her shoulder blades as he walked up to the bar. She was just two years his junior, and it had only taken a few minutes of simple conversation for the chemistry to mix between them and come alive.

The GPS on the car showed his arrival at the cottage. The gated driveway was already opened as he pulled up to the address. The driveway stretched up beyond the ornate wrought-iron gates and rose into the darkness of the heavily wooded area that lay shrouded in the October night. He turned into the driveway and proceeded.

The headlights of the car guided him through the night's murkiness as he slowly made his way up the winding road deeper into the trees. Abruptly, the cottage came into view on his left. The large house was dark and appeared empty. Louis had heard of this house in past conversations. An old two-story European cottage. Six bedrooms and two full baths, if he remembered Styles' bragging correctly. He pulled his car up the circular driveway and parked out front next to the house with the engine still idling. He glanced at the dashboard clock. 11: 19. Eleven minutes early. He turned the headlights off and waited.

At exactly 11:30, his phone rang. The number: Unknown Caller. He answered.

"Yes?"

"I see you arrived early. A man of punctuality, if nothing else," Styles stated.

"Where are you? Where's Cyndi?"

"Slow it down, Louis. I'm here at the cottage, as is Cynthia. I have a visual on you as we speak."

Louis turned and looked behind the car and began checking the rear- view mirrors for Styles. If he was standing nearby, it was too dark outside to tell. Not even the front porch light was left on. "Where are you?" He asked again.

"That is not relevant at this moment, Louis. Now do me a favour, and step out of your car and walk up onto the front porch, please?"

"Why?"

"Louis, we don't have all night for fifty questions. Please, if not for me, then for Cynthia. She's been waiting. Step out of your car."

Turning off the ignition, Louis stepped from the car. He glanced across the area in front of the house that was encircled by the wrap around driveway. The manicured grass held a decorative flowered garden with a tiny pond at its centre. The front lawn appeared empty as far as he could tell.

"The porch, Louis." Styles reminded him.

Turning his attention away from the front lawn, he ascended the stone stairs of the front porch. He stopped and turned back to the garden. He knew that somewhere, just out of his line of sight, Styles was standing in the shadows watching. Guiding him along like a dog on a leash.

"Now, do you see the mailbox," Styles began, "on the house near the front door? Inside, you'll find a simple flip phone. Leave yours in the mailbox and switch to the flip phone. We'll be using that from now on to speak."

Louis lifted the flap of the black metal mailbox and stuck the fingers of his free inside. He pulled out the flip phone.

"Now place yours inside. You'll have no use for that for the time being," Styles voice instructed.

Louis hesitated. "Why? What

difference does it make what phone I use?" Styles was trying to cover his tracks.

"Just do it, Louis. The more questions you bombard me with, the more time you're wasting. I'd like to get this done with as much as you do."

Louis sighed heavily. He did not like the idea of being separated from his phone. Especially when he knew Styles was up to something that would soon unfold. Against his better judgement, he ended the call and dropped his phone in the mailbox. As if on cue, the flip phone rang. Unknown caller.

"Now what?" Louis answered.

"Now you simply walk in, find Cynthia and listen to what she has to say. Oh, also, there is unfortunately no power available in the cottage, so I left you a candle and a flashlight on the table when you walk in. It's to your left."

"That's it?" Louis inquired, waiting for Styles to throw some additional requirement into this game of his.

"That's it. Plain and simple."

"How do I know you're—-" The phone cut off. He pulled it away from his ear. Styles had hung up on him in mid-sentence. Again, he had the last word. Louis looked over his shoulder and then tried dialling his own number. 'Outgoing Calls Blocked' came up on the screen, followed by a busy signal. That arrogant prick apparently thought of everything. Closing the phone, he slid it into his front pant pocket and tried the knob to the front door. It twisted, and the door opened inward. He stepped inside.

The interior was dark and obscured in thick shadows. The spacious foyer was cast in a greyish hue from the moonlight that attempted to enter from outside the opened door behind him. An archway to his left could be made out. Oak beams and brickwork were noticeable out in the hall as he passed through and entered the room on his left. He could make out the faint outline of a table in the dark due to the lunar gleam through the parted curtains of a window. He ambled forward, feeling about in the darkness until his hands came onto the smooth surface of the heavy table. He glided his fingers gently over the tabletop until he felt the flashlight. Grabbing it, he turned it on.

The beam of light basked the room in its illumination as he moved the light over his surroundings. He was in a dining room. The furniture about him was as rustic as the cottage itself. The furnishings were from a time whence the home was built. Crude yet of old-world construction. On the centre of the table, sat a large red candle. It was about a good ten to twelve inches high and almost conical. Thick at the base and tapering off to the slender tip. The candle was not of a smooth surface as your typical candle would have been moulded. This candle was carved into a piece of waxed art. Louis moved closer to examine the carvings in the red wax. In magnificent detail were multiple images of death. Adorning the candle's surface were etched skulls, skeletons, and gaunt humanoid creatures intertwined in a cadaverous orgy depicting the departure of life. A morbid looking candle if he ever beheld one. A small box of matches sat at its base.

Pulling a single wooden match from the box, he struck it and lit the black wick of the candle. Upon the lighting of the wick, a sickly sweet fetor resembling that of a sweltering trash heap filled the air around the eerie glow the flame gave off. Louis stepped back and grimaced at the odour. A smell as vile as the candle itself. He stepped away and moved back into the hall and closed the front door.

He played the beam of light about him, taking in the house's interior. It reminded him of a bed-and-breakfast he stayed at in

Maine a few years ago. First thing was first. He needed to find Cyndi and learn what Styles was up to. He called her name out in the dark. Nothing. Noticing a staircase to the second floor out in the foyer, he decided to start upstairs and work his way back down.

The old wooden stairs creaked unusually loud in the silent darkness as he ascended them. Pictures of Styles and Cyndi, along with other family members from both sides, along with social events they attended, hung from the wall going upstairs. He paused at one depicting the two making at toast while under a white gazebo in some flowered landscape. Cyndi was wearing a white form fitting dress. Louis gently caressed the image with the tips of his fingers. He thought of the first time he had made love to her in his apartment. He recalled how it had rained that night. He pulled his gaze away and continued up the stairs. He called her name again, and only the lingering stillness answered.

At the top of the stairs, he paused. *Did someone answer back in the dark?* He could have sworn he heard someone call out in a hushed tone as he climbed the last of the stairs.

"Cyndi? Are you there? It's Louis." He waited and listened. A floorboard creaked somewhere nearby. He moved the light around the second-floor landing and down the hall that led to the back of the house. An uneasy feeling was forming at the base of his skull. The hairs on his neck rose, and it caused him to shiver as his shoulder blades trembled and pulled back tightly. Something was not quite right. He could not see it, but he felt it. He continued down the hall, shunning the childish fear of the dark that plucked at his imagination. The ceiling was lower here. He raised his hand and slid his fingers along the beams overhead as he passed beneath them. 'We see you.' A voice whispered from behind him. He whirled and pointed the light back down the hall from where he had come. The corridor was empty. He realised that his jaw was tightening to where his teeth ached from the strain on them. He exhaled and tried to keep his breathing under control.

The phone vibrated in his pocket, causing him to jump. He quickly pulled it out and flipped it open.

"Yes?" Louis answered in frustration. Styles was getting the best of him with his ridiculous game being played out in the darkened house.

"Louis, are you alright? You sound…uneasy?"

"What is it, Styles? I'm about two minutes from telling you to go fuck yourself and going straight to the police."

Styles chuckled. "Come on, Louis. Don't tell me you're afraid of being in the dark? I left you a flashlight and the candle. Did you light the candle, Louis?"

"Yes. Why?"

"No reason. Just curious. Do you know

where I picked up that candle? No, of course you wouldn't. How could you? I picked that up in my travels to China, Louis. I had to travel for three days to a remote village in the upper regions of Northern China to obtain that candle."

"Like I give a flying fuck, Styles. I don't give a shit about the candle and to tell you what, it smells like shit too." He was actually glad to have received Styles' call. It drew his attention from his present surroundings and took the edge off. He felt the primitive fear ebb and his courage returning. He started down the hall and began opening the bedroom doors as he listened.

"There are priests in those villages who still practice the rites of the old ways.

They are hidden away from the modern world in areas so secluded and primitive that they make third world countries look like a thriving metropolis. They call the candles 'Death Candles.' Hand crafted by the high priest himself. They say the wax is stained red by the blood of newborn children, Louis."

The first bedroom consisted of twin beds and a dresser drawer. Nothing more. "Is that right? Tell those bullshit ghost stories to someone who cares. I'm not buying into it and if I don't find Cyndi in the next ten minutes, I'm going to the police."

"They refer to them as Death Candles." Styles continued paying Louis' threats no heed. "Because of what happens when they are lit. You did say you lit it, correct?"

The second bedroom contained a double bed and the same old-fashioned furnishings. No Cyndi. "Yes, so why don't you tell me what happens?"

"Once the candle is lit, it becomes a beckon. The flame can be seen by the natives of the netherworld. The Beckoning is what they referred to it as. It calls forth the sinister entities that reside in the realms of darkness and——-" Louis collapsed the phone and slid it back into his front pant pocket. "Shut the fuck up, Styles."

The third room was a bathroom. Unlike the two previous rooms, it was constructed with modern fittings. LED vanity lights fixed above the sink's mirror and a rainforest shower. 'We see you.' Came the hushed voice again from in the hall behind him. He spun and quickly pointed the flashlight's beam down both ends of the hall. Empty. He was getting that uneasy feeling again. He cursed himself for the immature frightfulness of being in the dark. If Styles could see him now, he'd relish in his unvaliant behaviour to no end.

There were two more doors left in the upper hall to check behind. He paused with his fingers on the doorknob to one room and listened. Was he hearing a fainting breathing? He held his own breath and listened again. Yes. He could make the faint sound of slow rasping breathing out. From the sound, whoever was producing the unpleasant noise, they weren't far from him. He again turned the beam of the flashlight back down the far end of the hall from where he had just come. The door to one of the far bedrooms was slightly opened. He distinctively recalled them all being closed. His heart pounded in his chest as he directed his attention to the door.

He held the light at the open door as he inched closer, but the light failed to penetrate the room's interior. Only a blackened void waited beyond the door. The breathing was no doubt coming from inside the room. He was sure of it! His mouth was rapidly drying as the saliva seemed to evaporate from his tongue. From somewhere within the room's depths, a shape blacker than the room itself shifted.

Was he now seeing a head peering at him from behind the door? A hand whose skin was as dark as the shrouded blackness that infested this house reached out from the void and gripped the door. It slowly began to open the door wider. "We see you," the figure inside whispered. Louis turned and fled down the hall.

He half stumbled down the flight of stairs as he ran down. He caught the railing midway down and stopped. He pointed the beam to the second landing and waited. Waited for the shape in the room to emerge into the light and show itself, but as he stood there on the stairs, nothing revealed itself to him. The laboured breathing itself was no more. He attempted to move his tongue about in his mouth to rid it of its arid condition and conjure up some trace of saliva. Sweat was forming on his forehead. He had enough of Styles' freak show! He bowed to the man's ingenious game and how it had caused him to be more afraid of the dark than being caught in bed with his wife.

He turned back to pictures on the wall. Seeing Cyndi's picture would reassure him just enough to run out of the house and to the authorities. His brow furled and mouth turned to a sickening frown as he moved the light closer to the picture of them under the gazebo. Styles' image remained the same, unaltered, but hers had changed. No longer was she the youthful, beautiful woman he had pulled from Style's demanding clutches. Her image was of a rotting corpse. Her skin now a dark sickening colour as the cadaver held the toasting pose with its face more skull than flesh. Louis moved the light over the other framed pictures. Each one containing Cyndi was now replaced with the festering corpse. It even managed a lipless smile in some photos. A floorboard in the landing above creaked, and he whipped the light up to sound. A tall, dark, lanky shape ducked quickly back into the hall, allowing him only a slight glimpse of its hairless form. He descended the remaining steps in two leaps.

He bounded into the foyer and rushed to the front door. His hands, however, fell only on a bricked wall. The door was no more. The same brick facing that designed the foyer now had taken over where the front door should have been. Louis' hands patted the wall repeatedly as he attempted to find a door which once was. This was impossible! It was as if a door never existed. Panic was overtaking him. From the room on his right where the light of the hideous candle illuminated, came a series of hushed voices speaking to each other. Their words undecipherable.

Still patting the wall as he moved, he made his way toward the open arch of the dining room. His eyes widened in horror as he stepped into the room. Seated at the head of the table across from him was a cloaked figure. The tattered black robe that clothed the form also included a dark cowl that covered the face that was hung down to the table. Its hands were laid out flat upon the table's surface. The hands that stretched from the sleeves were large and pale. Elongated fingers ending in black talons spread out. The candlelight filled the room with its repulsive odour and a display of flickering shadows that seemed to dance about in the gloom.

"You call upon the dark, yet you fear it." A voice, long dead and gravelled, said from under the cowl. Shapes began to manifest from the shadows. Twisted figures taking form only to whisper, 'We see you' before melding back into shadows. They seemed to fill the room. Some outstretching long gangly arms to touch Louis before retreating into the black nothingness.

Louis started backing out of the room. His eyes fix on the thing at the table as he slowly stepped backwards. He now noticed that the window on the wall was also no longer. Like the front door, it never existed. From behind him, a familiar voice called out his name.

He spun around to a new, more terrifying horror that stood in the foyer and began to slowly move into the light towards him. Its arms rose and outstretched themselves in an embracing gesture. Hands hanging with decayed flesh and long blackened nails reaching for him. "Louis, my love." It called out as it neared. The rotting cadaver that depicted Cyndi in the framed pictures stepped closer, causing Louis to step back into the dining room. His lips silently mouthing the word 'No' over and over. "I see you, Louis. I see you." It said to him as it advanced. The voices from the shadows repeating the verse. Her skin sagged and fell away in places. Her long blonde now white and tangle hung in loose patches of her skull head. One eye remained intact in the socket. Strips of meat dangled from the skull face.

Suddenly there were grasping hands upon him. The beings from the shadows were grabbing at him. Pulling at his hair, tearing at his clothes. Cadaver Cyndi was almost on him, her rotted skull-like face opening its mouth, revealing black, decayed teeth and a purple tongue. "Love me, Louis. Love me," it pleaded.

A scream was building inside his

throat as the dark hands found holdings on him, restraining him and pulling him to his knees. He felt his bladder give way and the hot urine pouring over him, staining his jeans.

The thing from the table lifted its head and turned to him. The face behind those burning red eyes showing itself to him. The scream inside Louis could no longer be contained and erupted from his throat in a long wail that burned his lungs. Cadaver Cyndi was now on him, wrapping her bony arms around his neck, her long, black nails digging into him. Her rotted mouth pressing itself onto his, muffling his scream as the hideous tongue slid into his mouth. The two fell to the floor as long black limbs pulled them into the growing shadows of the abyssal vortex.

"To call upon death, one must be willing to accept it when it comes," the thing at the table said as it stood. The candlelight faded as the room was slowly plunged into the inevitable blackness and engulfed all.

***

Outside the cottage, Styles heard the terrifying scream from within the building's lightless confines as it echoed in the chilled night air. He stood leaning against his burgundy-coloured Mercedes parked just inside the far tree line, his hands in the pockets of his leather coat. As he stood staring at the cottage and pondering how Louis had met his fate, he also wondered why the man hadn't come rushing out of the front door when the powers summoned made themselves fully present. It would be the logical course of action. It's what he would have done. Never-the-less, he had seen the last of the man and would wait until morning to enter the cottage. Taking the flip phone from his pocket it, he gave it one last look before tossing it into the trees, hearing it land in the underbrush somewhere out in the darkness.

He sighed briefly, then reached into his other pocket and produced a similar phone. He flipped it open and held it to his ear. It rang twice before someone answered it.

"Cynthia, darling. Are you okay? You seem stressed. No. No. Louis will be at the shore house soon. I promise. Yes. Yes. By the way, did you light the candle I left for you? Good. Good. Well, just sit back and relax. Things should start getting interesting very soon, I promise."

NOT AT REST

By Galina Trefil

Billy was tickled that Giles, the mean old man next door, was buried here in such a remote, run-down location. Most graves were over a century old. No one ever came to visit. No one would see a vandal sneaking in after midnight.

Laughing, Billy knocked down Giles' freshly erected tombstone with a sledgehammer.

He didn't hear the tombstone behind him shaking. He didn't realise that it was starting to fall until…*crunch.* Now he lay pinned in the dirt, struggling for breath.

The critters and bugs would come to eat him soon. Wearing an invisible smirk, Giles looked forward to watching.

REMEMBRANCE

By Helen Merrick

"There's rosemary, that's for remembrance"—*Hamlet*, William Shakespeare

She jolted awake, uncertain why. Fists clenching the blankets, she listened. Her heart raced, pounded her chest as if desperate to escape. Sweat beaded her brow. Her nightdress was clammy and a chill draught raised goosebumps on the flesh beneath. Gwen shivered but dare not reach for the fluffy nightgown curled on the bedside chair like a sleeping cat. She held her breath, listened intently. The wind howled, whistling around the chimney, and the house creaked. But that wasn't it. That wasn't the disturbance.

There. She tensed. Footsteps—soft, steady footfalls—and the creak of stairs. Trembling, she pulled the blankets up to her face. She cowered, peering into the darkness, straining to see movement, but seeing nothing. The footsteps ceased. Silence. Then the door squeaked on rusty hinges, slowly opening.

"Who's there?"

Gwen's strangled voice was little more than a whisper, but the door's progress halted. All was still. No sounds other than the house's protests at the raging storm and the element's cruel response. Then she heard the voice, distinct and clear above the whistling wind, *"Leah..."*

***

Gwen sat bolt upright, eyes wide. She gasped but, blinking at daylight, slowly exhaled. Sinking back onto her pillows, she watched the sun play hide and seek behind the clouds. Its periodically peeping face penetrated the thin cotton curtains, throwing geometric patterns over the room only to snatch them back again. Gwen clasped her quivering hands. The memory of the nightmare lingered, fear lurking in her chest, its head pressed heavy against her stomach.

Too scared to leave her bed, she listened: the storm had passed and a quieter, calmer world lay beyond her windows. The wind, so angry in the night, whispered teasingly to the trees and tickled their branches. Birdsong carried above the rustle, shrill and joyful. Reassured, Gwen crept from her bed and drew back the curtains. The sky was gun-metal grey and clouds moved faster than the hushed breeze had suggested. *Still miserable.* She hated October: everything dying, days getting darker, colder, shorter.

Lowering her gaze, she noticed a dog-eared curl of wallpaper beneath the windowsill. She pulled it, frowning as a large section peeled back to reveal bare plaster. Gwen shook her head. It wasn't the only peeling paper she'd found recently. Making a mental note to fix it, she shuffled off to the bathroom to wash.

She was dressing when the whine of a drill shattered the peace. The piercing squeal hurt her ears and vibrations shook the mirror on the wardrobe door. Gwen grimaced. *Next door.* She'd never wanted a semi-detached house, and this was why. At least Mrs Green had been quiet. Shame she'd moved out—relocated to an old people's home, of all places. Gwen shuddered. She was never leaving her home. She clamped hands over her ears until the drilling stopped. There was a peaceful hiatus before hammering took its place.

Gwen hadn't met her new neighbours and wondered who they were. Next door had been vacant for a while, the For Sale sign only recently removed, and she hadn't noticed anyone move in. It was nice to have neighbours again.

"I hope they're not always this loud," she muttered as the drilling resumed.

***

Gwen shuddered. The footfalls were distinct. Sound carried from next door? Maybe it had been them the previous night, too? She'd often heard Mrs Green moving around at night, but with the house empty for so long, she'd forgotten the noises neighbours could make. *Yes, that must be it. Either that or I'm dreaming.*

The dark clouds had dispersed over the course of the day, the clearer skies allowing sporadic moonlight to cast a dim glow through the bedroom curtains. The hands on the wall clock were illuminated enough to read—two-forty in the morning. Gwen tugged at her blankets and curled on her side. Screwing her eyes tight, she willed herself to sleep.

"Leah, Leah..."

The voice sounded close. Gwen banged on the wall. That would let the neighbours know she could hear.

"Leah, sweetheart..."

She banged again, then gasped as she felt the lightest caress upon her forehead, like a breath of wind. The mattress dipped beside her and she heard a soft sigh.

"Leah, why did you leave?"

Gwen froze: ears burning, eyes searching. "Who's there? What do you want?"

The mattress sprang back, and the voice ceased. Shaken, Gwen lay awake while the wall clock counted the minutes and chimed the hours.

***

She spotted him raking leaves in the garden. He was a short, stocky man, but his face was quite attractive and his floppy, unkempt hair had boyish appeal. He appeared to be alone, no sign of anyone who could be *Leah*. She got a better look as he moved closer to the house, then huffed when he climbed over the fence and started raking leaves on her side.

Gwen rapped on the window. "You don't need to do that," she shouted. "I can look after my own garden." The man looked up, alarmed, and dived back over the fence. "Oh, dear..." Gwen waved guiltily. "It's okay, I'm not cross." But he was gone.

There was no drilling or hammering that day, but Gwen could hear her neighbour pacing and talking—on the phone, perhaps? When she heard his back door open, she rushed to the window to speak to him, but he kept close to the house, out of sight. So much for friendly new neighbours.

The knock on the door came late afternoon.

"Andy," he said, tentatively offering his hand. "I own…"

"Next door, I know." Gwen met his startled gaze. "I'm sorry if I scared you. I didn't mean to sound angry. I'm Gwen. Gwen Roberts."

Andy gaped. His arm fell limply to his side. "Roberts?"

"That's right."

He stared at her, brow crinkling. Then his eyebrows shot up his forehead. "Gwendolyn Roberts?"

"So, you've heard of me?" She smiled. "Gwen, please. No one calls me Gwendolyn."

"Right," he said, shifting uncomfortably. "Good to meet you, Gwen." He continued to stare, and Gwen couldn't help noticing how blue his eyes were, like the sky in summer. "Look, I erm, I just popped round to… but now I really should…"

"Oh, yes, you go." Gwen nodded. "You must be busy, you and your girlfriend. Leah, isn't it?"

Andy slowly shook his head. "No girlfriend. Just me."

"Oh? My mistake." Gwen's stomach contracted and she grasped the doorframe as a wave of nausea sent her head spinning.

"You okay?" Concern showed in his bright eyes.

"Yes, I'm fine. Bit tired."

"Okay, I'll leave you to rest." Andy took a step back, then faltered. "Sorry about the noise. I'm renovating the house." He drew breath, as if he had more to say. Instead, he pointed to his house. "I have to…"

"Yes, I understand. Call in any time." Gwen bit her lip as she closed the door. No Leah. The voice hadn't carried from next door. The *presence* was real.

***

It was cold, so cold. The central heating pipes were singing, but the hot water flowing through their innards wasn't enough to dispel the chill. The wind had whipped up again and a steady downpour drummed a military tattoo on the roof tiles. *Two-forty.* Nervous of being woken, but thirsty, Gwen slipped on her dressing gown and headed downstairs to put the kettle on. She moved cautiously, alert for alien sounds and any movement in the shadows. While the kettle boiled on the hob, she stared at the wallpaper. The golden floral pattern didn't quite match at the joins, and a peeling edge reminded her that she still hadn't fixed the patch in the bedroom.

Gwen took her tea into the living room. With the standard lamp casting a warm glow, and sipping hot tea, her shivering lessened. Yet she could still feel the cold, and the hairs on the back of her neck prickled. She looked around, half expecting to find someone there, watching unseen.

"Leah..."

She jolted, tea slopping over her mug. The voice was right beside her.

"Leah, sweetheart…"

"Who's there?" Gwen sprang to her feet, clutching the mug tightly. She cast around wildly but saw no one. Then a strange scent invaded her nostrils—faint at first, then stronger. Food? Cooking? Who was cooking at this time of night? The stairs creaked, and a shiver ran down her spine, cold as ice.

"Show yourself," she said, summoning her strength. "I know you're here."

"Leah, come back to me, we belong together. Remember…"

Gwen dropped the mug. Tea scalded her bare feet and she cried out. It was then that she noticed the cut-glass vase on the coffee table in front of her. A sprig of greenery protruded from it. Gwen screamed, "No!"

Suddenly the room vibrated as if shaken by an earthquake. Fat sofa cushions tumbled to the floor, the windows rattled violently. The vase tipped, shattering into vicious shards, its contents spilt. Shrieking, Gwen fled. She ran full tilt toward the bedroom, tripping on the stairs in her haste. Her right knee struck the edge of a step and she yelped in pain but, grabbing the bannister, hauled herself upright and carried on.

"Leah, why did you leave?" the voice called, louder now.

"Go away! Leave me alone."

"Leah, remember... remember... remember..."

Diving into bed, Gwen recoiled beneath the blankets. She hugged her knees and rocked as the voice died away, leaving her in the company of the howling wind.

***

"Hi again, remember me?"

Gwen flinched at his words.

"Oh, bad timing?" Andy was on her doorstep, smile fading. "I thought I'd pop round to... I'm a bit embarrassed about yesterday."

"Not bad timing, no. Sorry." She forced a smile. "You did seem a little shy."

"Yeah," he gave a strange hiccupping laugh, "surprised, more like. I thought this house was empty, see. The Estate Agents misled me."

"Did they, indeed?"

Andy grimaced. "They told me both these houses were vacant, but…" He gestured to Gwen. "Here you are. And I'm very pleased to meet you," he added, bobbing his head. "Properly, that is."

"Likewise." Gwen hesitated. "Would you like to come in?"

"Erm, yes."

Gwen opened the door wide and led Andy to her living room, where she patted the cream and blue sofa. "Take a seat. Tea?"

"No, thank you. I mustn't stay long." Andy gazed around. "The rooms look so different with furniture in."

"I'll bet. You said you're renovating

next door," said Gwen, lowering herself into her high-backed armchair. "Doing what, exactly?"

"Refurbishment.   Modernisation. Nothing much actually."

Gwen nodded. "Mrs Green kept it nice. Did you know she had it rewired a few years back?"

"I did, yes." He looked at Gwen's faded blue floral wallpaper and scuffed skirting. "Your house looks untouched."

"Untouched but not unloved," said Gwen. "The previous owner put this paper up and it's peeling, but shh…" She placed a finger to her lips. "It's not too noticeable."

"No, no, I like it. No photos," he commented. "I always expect to see photos or portraits on living room walls."

Gwen shrugged. "I've no family, so the only photographs would be of me, and I'm not especially photogenic."

"Oh, I don't know." Andy smiled. His face was kind, his smile warm. "I can show you what I've done next door, if you like." He tapped his phone and handed it to her. The pictures showed a mirror image of her house stripped bare: floors bereft of carpet, walls newly plastered. "They're a good size, these semis, with fantastic gardens. They don't build them like this anymore. New-builds are awful, much smaller."

"Really?" Gwen looked around. "I thought this was small. Of course, having fields out back is rather lovely. And all the beautiful beech trees."

"Fields?"

"Behind the house." She passed the phone to Andy.

"Right. Yes." He smiled awkwardly, then glanced at his watch. "I should, erm… I want to get some more done before I go home."

"Home?" Gwen tilted her head, a stray lock falling over her face. "You've not moved in?" she asked, pushing the hair back into place.

"No. The house is a project. I'll sell it when I'm done."

"Oh, I see." She clutched her stomach, which felt strangely heavy. "So you're a temporary neighbour?"

"I am." Andy smiled, and Gwen instinctively stared at his bright blue eyes.

"Well, I'd better go," he said. "Are you okay? You look pale."

"Do I?" Gwen held his gaze. "I didn't sleep well. You—you weren't next door last night, were you? By any chance?"

"No. I left at eight." His brows furrowed, meeting in the middle. "Why? Did something…" He hesitated, mouth twisting. "Did something keep you awake?"

Lowering her gaze, Gwen fidgeted.

"You can tell me," he said, softly.

Gwen pursed her lips. Images of her nightmares formed, needing to be shared. She sucked in a breath. "Noises. Voices, actually."

Andy nodded, showing no sign of surprise. "I guess voices carry through these walls. But it wasn't me last night."

"No." Gwen sighed. "Look, I'm tired."

"Of course. I'll go." Andy shuffled forward, then sat back again. "Can I ask, have you lived here long?"

"Nearly fifty years."

"Fifty? But you didn't buy the house new?"

"No. It was built around twenty years before I moved in," she said. "Why?"

"Because…" Andy faltered. "Okay, I'll come straight out with it. I've heard things too, through the walls. Noises. Voices. And I've talked to other neighbours." He leaned forward. "They say this house is, well… *haunted*."

"Haunted?" Gwen laughed. "My house, haunted? Which neighbours told you that? They're winding you up."

"So, the name Leah doesn't mean anything to you?"

Gwen gasped. A lump formed in her throat—burning, choking.

"I can see from your face that it does. Your house is haunted by Leah and Daniel. Previous occupants, apparently."

Gwen tittered nervously. "I don't think so. Someone's having you on."

"Maybe, but Leah died last year and several of the neighbours swear they've spotted her since. Goodness, you do look peaky. Can I get you anything?" When Gwen shook her head, Andy stood. "Just one more thing." He fished a scrap of paper from inside his overalls. "I've got some paint left over, this colour." He offered the remnant to Gwen. "I reckon it would look good in here."

"In here?"

Andy nodded. "You said the wallpaper was peeling, so why don't I re-decorate? I'm happy to do it."

Gwen took the paper and held it against her tired wallpaper. *Cornflower blue.* "It would look lovely." She bit her lip. "I can't pay you."

"I don't want money," he said. "It'll be my pleasure. Do I have your permission?"

Gwen thought for a moment, then smiled warmly. "Yes, you do."

***

The greenery in the vase had been a sprig of rosemary, and finding another piece laid on her pillow threw Gwen into a panic. Tears streaming down her face, she opened the window and tossed the sprig into the stormy night. The harsh wind attacked her hair and stung her skin, but the cold felt good. Felt real.

"Leah..."

Gwen spun around. Guttural sobs choking her, she wailed, "Leave me alone, I'm not Leah. I'm Gwen."

The stifling aroma of cooking filled the room, smells that couldn't waft in on the wind at this hour of night. Sweet herbs, roast meat, delicious scents that rotted in an instant, making Gwen heave. "Go away, leave me alone."

She covered her eyes and prayed for the storm to sweep through the room, blowing away the offensive odours and hateful voice. To her surprise, it obliged. The curtains billowed as the wind howled past like a rabid beast, shaking everything in its path. The bedclothes were tossed asunder, the chair tipped, and Gwen's flesh was slapped by the icy blast. She stood shaking at the centre of the maelstrom, but a triumphant smile tugged at her lips.

***

Noises downstairs awakened her: a door banging, whistling? Nightgown hastily donned, Gwen tiptoed downstairs. A man was in her living room, a paint tin in his hand.

"Andy?"

"Jeez!" The tin slipped to the floor with a bang. "You scared me." Andy bent to retrieve it. "It's okay, the lid stayed on so no harm done."

No harm? Gwen seethed. "What are you doing in my house?"

"Decorating." He shrugged. "Like we agreed."

"While I'm asleep in bed? How did you get in?"

"The front door wasn't locked." He looked sheepish. "I did knock and call out." He put the paint tin on the coffee table. "Do you want me to leave?"

"Yes, I most certainly—" A familiar whiff caught Gwen's attention. The hairs on the back of her neck rose. "Do you smell that?" she asked.

"Smell what?" Andy sniffed. "Oh yeah, lovely. Someone's having roast dinner, lucky them. I love a good roast, don't you? Roast lamb with all the trimmings. Beautiful."

Gwen baulked. Something in the back of her mind stirred and a stabbing pain shot through both temples. She winced, the memory slipping from her grasp. "Go, please," she said, gingerly touching her forehead. "You can paint another day."

Andy didn't argue. "I'll show myself out."

***

The sprig of rosemary hovered in the air above her, turning slowly. Fascinated, Gwen watched it slowly grow, sprouting new shoots, new leaves. Then it bloomed with delicate blue flowers. The stems expanded, leaves doubled in number, then doubled again. They multiplied like bacteria on an agar plate until the bedroom was filled with pungent rosemary, choking her, squeezing the breath from her lungs.

"Leah."

Gwen grasped her blankets and drew them close. The vision vanished, but her fear didn't. Heart pounding, she listened.

"Leah, why did you leave?"

"Go away, I'm not Leah."

"Oh, Leah, remember…"

To Gwen's horror, a face materialised in the gloom, its distorted features illuminated by an unearthly light. A shadowy hand, glistening like ice crystals, reached out. The fingers opened to reveal a tiny sprig of rosemary. "No! Get that away from me." Gwen lashed out, slashing the air with flailing arms, thrashing wildly until the image was obliterated. Out of breath, she panted. "This stops, now. No more."

***

The house looked beautiful: cornflower blue paint with crisp white ceilings and new cream carpets. The windows had been given a new coat of gloss and the skirting looked immaculate. Impressed, Gwen handed the phone back to Andy.

"And you could paint this room like that?" she asked.

"Absolutely." He sat back, hugging a cushion. "In fact, I could do the whole house."

Gwen shook her head. "I've already said I can't pay."

"I know."

"Then why…" She noticed the colour rising in Andy's cheeks and the way he fidgeted. "What's going on? What do you want?"

"Nothing. I thought you might like—"

"I would," she interrupted. "But what's in it for you?"

Andy sighed. He put the cushion down. "Okay, okay… I've finished next door so now I want to get this house done."

"Done? What do you mean, *done*?"

"Renovated. So I can sell it. Sell them both, if anyone will buy them. Which I doubt, with you here."

Gwen narrowed her eyes. "What are you talking about?"

"You won't leave so I found a way to work around you—thought I'd found a way." Andy looked her in the eyes, his voice earnest. "Gwen, sweet Gwen, look out of the window. What do you see?"

"You know what I can see," she said curtly, without turning.

"Fields and beech trees."

"That's right, yes."

"Look, Gwen. Actually *look*," Andy pleaded. "The only beech tree is the one in your garden and there are no fields. It's all gone. Has been for years. There's nothing but houses and concrete. Little houses, boxy ones. The sort I don't like, remember?"

"Out there? Rubbish," Gwen retorted. "Don't talk such rot."

"Gwen," Andy spoke softly, "you're seeing what you want to see."

"No," Gwen shook her head again, "you're wrong. You're mad!" She flapped her hands at him. "Get out. Leave before I call the police." But the sound of crashing trees echoed in her mind and she could hear the drone of diggers and earthmovers. *No, no…it's not real. They're not falling.* "The trees are shedding their autumn leaves," she said aloud.

"Houses and concrete. And it's the middle of summer."

Gwen looked up, tears stinging her eyes.

"I did some research." Andy held his phone out to Gwen. "I hate to do this to you, I really do. But you have to see this. Please," he coaxed.

Uncertain, Gwen looked. The phone

showed a copy of a death certificate. *Daniel Andrew Roberts died August 5th 1979.*

"Who's this?" she asked, weakly. "The man who's haunting me?"

"Yes. Your husband."

"My *what?*" Gwen felt sick. Blood rushed in her ears.

"You're Gwendolyn Ophelia Roberts. Daniel's wife."

She shook her head adamantly. "I'd remember if… I'd…" Pain shot through her brain—burning, stinging—and something spikey irritated her palm. Opening her hand, she found a tiny sprig of rosemary. "T-this," she stammered, holding it out. "What's this?"

Andy leaned toward her. "That's

rosemary," he said, "for remembrance."

Remember... The voice echoed in her mind. "Did you plant *this* in my vase?" she cried. "Did you put some in my bedroom?"

Andy shook his head. "What happened to Daniel, Gwen?"

"I don't know."

"Tell me, please, I want to help. I want you to find peace."

"I am at peace," Gwen protested. But his words cut deep, severing the cords that secured her cruellest memories and prevented their surfacing. It was like a veil lifting or fog blown away by the wind. Clarity. Remembrance.

"He wouldn't call me Gwendolyn," she whispered, not knowing where the words were coming from, or how to control the surge of emotions unleashing inside her. "He didn't like Gwendolyn, and Gwen was too *common*." Memories bubbled from her subconscious depths and exploded into consciousness. Blind panic battling with truth, she trembled as she spoke. "I didn't like Ophelia, so we settled on Leah. Oh, God…"

"What happened, Gwen?"

Her head hurt dreadfully: so many images and feelings, tattered, torn and twisted together like debris in a storm. "We were happy." She rubbed her forehead. "I remember his face—kind, a warm smile. And beautiful eyes. He bought both these houses; planned to do them up and sell them."

"Like me. Go on."

"He finished next door. Lovely, it was." She turned to the paint tin on the coffee table where Andy had left it. "Walls that colour, white woodwork. We sold it to Jane Green."

"And this house?"

A fat tear rolled down Gwen's cheek. "He never even started renovating this one. Lost interest. He took a desk job in town, bought a flat near work while I moved me in here. I barely saw him."

"And how did he die?"

Gwen shook her head.

"Please, Gwen. Tell me."

Gwen wiped her palms on her housecoat. Andy looked sincere. *Okay. Why not?* She inhaled. "He came home every Saturday, sometimes late, so I'd cook

Sunday lunch for him, try to make it special. He loved a roast, especially lamb. He liked to have all the trimmings—mint sauce, gravy. And it had to be cooked with a sprig of rosemary on top. I grew it in the garden specially. If I ever forgot," she paused, bit her lip.

"Oh, Gwen, did he hurt you?"

"Not physically. He shouted, criticised my cooking, criticised everything. And I was so naïve; I couldn't understand why he didn't love me. Until I found out." She tensed. "It doesn't matter now," she said, her voice suddenly cold. "He got what was coming to him."

"Did he? How?"

"The rosemary. He choked on it." Her lips twitched and stretched into an odd, crooked half-smile. "Can you imagine? It was quite bizarre. I cooked a roast dinner on the hottest day of the year, and not only did he eat it, but he choked on a tiny bit of rosemary stuck to the meat." Her smile became a cruel smirk. "I couldn't believe my luck."

Andy gaped.

"Of course, I could have helped him, slapped him on the back or something. But I didn't." She shrugged. "I went for a walk and left him to it. He was cold when I got back—cold as the remains of his dinner. Or as cold as he could get on a day that warm."

"Oh, my God."

"A friend told me about his affairs, you see, and the wild nights out. Seems he bragged about his antics, saying he married too young and couldn't live out the rest of his life with, and I quote, *that dowdy little woman.*" Gwen sighed. "He was sweet when we met, and shy, with such a kind face. Then he made me feel worthless."

"I'm so sorry," Andy whispered.

"Don't be. I was happy once he'd gone." She looked around and nodded appreciatively. "I have a happy life here. I can't complain at all." She turned her gaze back to Andy. "Do you think he'll leave me alone now I've confessed?"

"I don't know. I hope so."

"Hmm. One thing I don't understand," she said, frowning. "Why does he haunt me at night? He died in the afternoon, so why the obsession with two-forty in the morning? I don't get the significance."

"Ah…" Andy looked at his hands and picked at a spot of dried paint. "I…er…think that may have been *your* time of death."

A chill pierced Gwen to the bone, like the wind had blown right through her.

"Gwendolyn Ophelia Roberts passed away peacefully in her sleep in the early hours of October thirtieth, twenty-seventeen," said Andy. "Your obituary's online." He tapped his phone again and held it out.

"No." Gwen shook her head vehemently.

"*Both* houses were vacant, and I bought them."

"Liar!" Gwen stood, shoulders back. She pointed a finger. "I know what you're doing and you're not getting me out of this house."

"I'm not doing anything."

"Liar," she shouted. "Getting me to admit to letting my husband die, trying to get me arrested or…or committed."

"I'm doing no such thing. I own this house. Look at this, Gwen. Look." Andy thrust his phone at her again, but she knocked it from his hands. "No, you need to remember," he said, retrieving it. "You've both passed."

Gwen's head pounded. Memories whirled, burst open, the truth screaming to be heard. "I know," she cried. "I know." She glared at Andy, and something about the way he pushed his hair away from his eyes awakened more memories. Deeper ones—those she'd wanted to stay buried. *Oh.* She pointed and the crooked smile recaptured her face. "Now, that is funny."

Andy blinked. "Pardon?"

"Why are you here?" Gwen asked, her voice calm.

"You know why I'm here."

"To paint my house?"

"My house, actually."

"Right, your house." Gwen laughed. "That's not why you're here."

"What?" Andy scowled. "What are you—"

"Why do you need to know what happened? Why I left Daniel and went for that walk?" Gwen smiled. "Come on, I'm interested. Why is it important?"

"Because I want peace. For you."

Gwen watched him, amused. "Really? Look in your pockets, Andy."

"What?"

"Go on. Humour me. Look in your pockets." Annoyed, Andy stood and delved into his overalls. Gwen watched his bemused expression as he drew out a sprig of rosemary. "You only see what you want to," she said, her smile stretching her mouth in a clown-like grimace. "And I gave you permission to be here. Silly me."

Dumb-struck, Andy gawked.

"Oh, don't look like that. You called me Leah, so I called you *Andy*. Remember? Bet the neighbours had a fright seeing you at their doors. Or not. I don't suppose they remember you. Too long ago."

"What are you on about?" Andy took

a step away. "What…you think I'm Daniel?"

"Daniel Andrew—"

"You're mad," he said, edging toward the door.

"Probably. And *dead*, according to you." Gwen clicked her tongue and pointed to the window. The wind was shaking leaves from the beech tree in the garden and the heavy grey sky threatened rain. She wagged a finger. "Definitely October. I hate October."

"What the…"

"Go home every night, do you? And where's that, Andy?"

"My flat in the city." He clutched his head. "No, damn it, don't look like… I'm not him."

"Really?" Gwen chuckled. "Well, *Andy,* my answer is yes."

"Yes?" He stared.

"Yes, you can redecorate the whole house. Be my guest. Rejuvenate, refurbish, to your heart's content. Make it look beautiful." She moved closer. "Like you promised years ago."

"No!" With the sound of her laughter ringing in his ears, Andy blundered from the room. "I'm not Daniel," he cried as he flung the front door open.

Andy froze. There was nothing outside. Nothing but darkness.

HE WASN'T THERE

By Joel R. Hunt

Re: The Godwin Case—progress?

From: asherniazi@nhs.net

To: green.em@pattontrust.org

Date: 22/05/17

Hello Emily,

I was just wondering if you'd made any progress with Felicity Godwin? Peter's been sharing more with me in session, but his account is somewhat scattered, and I think some cross-referencing may shed light on what he's telling me. In any event, we should definitely organise a meeting before the first court date, preferably a week in advance to give Defence a good time to process it all.

Kind regards,

Asher

Dr Asher Niazi, Child Psychiatrist

Re: The Godwin Case—progress?

From: green.em@pattontrust.org

To: asherniazi@nhs.net

Date: 22/05/17

Hi Asher,

Funny you should email me today—3 hours ago Felicity spoke to me for the first time since we started therapy! And we definitely do need to cross-reference, because what she said got me worried; Peter and Felicity definitely haven't been in contact, have they? I think she referenced him, but I'm not 100% sure.

She said—or more whispered—"He doesn't like all these questions."

I tried to probe who she meant, because that was literally all she said, but she wouldn't give me anything more. I could only conclude that she meant Peter and your counselling, but how would she know his opinion on it? Am I just projecting onto her, do you think, with our personal contact making me presume it was about Peter?

Anyway, that's all I've got out of her in 4 weeks.

Tuesday 13th good for you for the meet-up? (June, obviously)

Thanks,

Emily

Dr Emily Green, Lead Psychiatrist with The Patton Trust

Re: The Godwin Case—progress?

From: asherniazi@nhs.net

To: green.em@pattontrust.org

Date: 22/05/17

Hello Emily,

No, to my knowledge there has been no contact between the two of them. In fact, Peter has been quite insistent on my confirming Emily's safety. He refused to talk to me until I could show him a picture of her that had been taken since they've been split up. That was why I requested one from your office a few weeks ago.

It stands to reason, I think, that if they were somehow colluding, he wouldn't have needed that reassurance.

The 13th sounds good, I'll check my

schedule and we'll organise a time tomorrow.

Best of luck with Felicity, it sounds like I got the more talkative twin!

Kind regards,

Asher

Dr Asher Niazi, Child Psychiatrist

Re: The Godwin Case—progress?

From: green.em@pattontrust.org

To: asherniazi@nhs.net

Date: 23/05/17

Morning Asher,

6pm okay for the meeting? I can travel to you if that's easier.

Felicity refusing to come in today—again—so I'm thinking I'll spend that time reviewing the case background. Do you have your I.P.A. of Peter?

Thanks,

Emily

Dr Emily Green, Lead Psychiatrist with The Patton Trust

Re: The Godwin Case—progress?

From: asherniazi@nhs.net

To: green.em@pattontrust.org

Date: 23/05/17

Hello Emily,

Hah! Finished at six pm on a weekday, eh? I don't care how many of your hours you're volunteering, that charity gig is spoiling you!

I can do after eight in the afternoon or maybe a rushed morning meeting before eight am. Or we could fit it into a lunch break? How's half twelve for you?

I'll send the assessment document shortly.

Yours overworkedly,

Asher

Dr Asher Niazi, Child Psychiatrist

P.G. Initial Assessment – CONFIDENTIAL

From: asherniazi@nhs.net

To: green.em@pattontrust.org

Date: 23/05/17

Hello Emily,

Peter's I.P.A. attached.

Confidential, obviously. Please don't make copies beyond your work email; that'd have to come through formal request.

Regards,

Asher

Dr Asher Niazi, Child Psychiatrist

Attached (1)OpenDownload

INITIAL PSYCHIATRIC ASSESSMENT REPORT

NAME OF PATIENT: *Peter Godwin*

DATE OF BIRTH: *18–02–2006*

GENDER: *Male*

ASSESSOR: *Dr Asher Niazi*

DATE OF ASSESSMENT: *27–04–2017*

CAUSE FOR REFERRAL: *Peter Godwin (herein "Peter" or "The patient") was discovered by police at his own home alongside the deceased bodies of his parents (Andrew Godwin and Melissa Godwin). Peter was covered in blood and in a state of significant agitation. Peter's twin sister (Felicity Godwin, herein "Felicity") was discovered in a similar* *state. Neither Peter nor Felicity were able to provide explanation of the events leading up to the deaths of their parents, and the pair were removed to two distinct, secure locations. Arresting officers speculate Peter may have killed his parents, and both twins have been referred to separate psychiatrists for an assessment prior to being charged with murder. At the point of writing, neither have formally confessed or denied guilt.*

***ASSESSMENT:** The patient expresses continual and severe agitation, including aggressive shouting and movements, though has currently not progressed to acts of physical violence against myself or others. Peter has so far refused to engage with the therapy sessions being offered to* *him, and his levels of anxiety are significantly increased by questions of any form, especially those regarding his parents or sister. In the hour of my initial observation, the only lucid statement that was made by the patient was: "He wasn't there." This was repeated by the patient at least twelve times by my own estimation, though on discussion the officers present and his legal representative (Mrs Kay Wright) it appears that this statement ("He wasn't there") has been continually used since the patient was first discovered alongside his deceased parents. So far there is little indication who the "He" being referred to is.*

INITIAL CONCLUSION: *The patient may pose a risk to himself or others, though* *it is not immediately apparent to me that he is expressing indications of guilt or malevolent intent; much of Peter's behaviour is in line with an individual suffering from severe trauma, which in this instance may have been caused by, rather than been the cause of, the death of his parents.*

I accept and second the recommendation of the Crown Prosecution that Peter and his sister be kept apart from one another and not allowed to engage in unobserved contact, both to ensure their own safety and to prevent collusion, intentional or otherwise.

Re: P.G. Initial Assessment - CONFIDENTIAL

From: green.em@pattontrust.org

To: asherniazi@nhs.net

Date: 23/05/17

Asher,

Gratefully received. Lunchtime is absolutely fine for the meeting, if you think we can compare notes in half an hour.

Thanks,

Emily

Dr Emily Green, Lead Psychiatrist with The Patton Trust

Re: P.G. Initial Assessment - CONFIDENTIAL

From: green.em@pattontrust.org

To: asherniazi@nhs.net

Date: 26/05/17

Hello Asher,

I think we need to bring forward our meeting.

I finally got Felicity to come back today, and something significant happened. I was asking her if anyone had been in contact with her parents before the police had arrived (I have been attempting to avoid direct reference to their deaths, so focussing on events leading up to it instead). After 47 seconds of silence—I know it was that long because I listened back to the recording several times before writing this—Felicity told me that "He wasn't there." I asked who she meant, and she didn't reply, but then I specifically asked if she meant Peter. She shook her head. I asked—I'll quote here—"Then who do you mean? Who is 'he'?" After that, she cried for half an hour.

Given both Felicity and Peter's statements about an unidentified "he," it is my current belief that someone else was involved in the murder of the Godwins. I believe the children may have witnessed it and are now scared to provide any more details. I'm passing these statements on to the police, and I think we both need to work to see if we can get a description of this person out of Felicity and Peter.

Emily

Dr Emily Green, Lead Psychiatrist with The Patton Trust

Re: P.G. Initial Assessment - CONFIDENTIAL

From: <u>asherniazi@nhs.net</u>

To: <u>green.em@pattontrust.org</u>

Date: 26/05/17

Hello Emily,

I understand your concern. I definitely think it is a possibility we must explore, and I utterly back your actions so far, though I'm hesitant to leap to any conclusions just yet. My current theory is that the children may be referring to a fictional or imaginary figure, one that Peter has recently taken to calling "The Man." There have been studies regarding the sharing of intense imaginary experiences between twins, which would explain the combined references to this figure, and I wonder if Peter is using The Man as justification, or perhaps as blame, for his own actions.

Just think about that phrase they both use. "He wasn't there." I think it's unlikely this is referring to a killer, who most certainly *would* have been there, and it can't be in reference to Peter himself, or else Peter wouldn't be using third person.

Naturally this is confidential, but I've attached a recording from one of our recent sessions. The moment of interest begins at around thirty-five minutes and twenty seconds in. I've transcribed it below:

PETER: He wasn't there.

ME: Who? (Silence) The Man?

PETER: Yes.

ME: Then where was he? (Silence) Peter, where was The Man?

PETER: He wasn't there.

ME: Have you ever seen The Man, Peter?

PETER: Yes.

ME: And you saw him somewhere else?

PETER: No. I saw him in my house. I saw him not be there.

ME: I'm not sure I understand. (Silence) You say you saw him, Peter? (Silence) Do you see him often?

PETER: Yes.

ME: Have you ever seen him here? (Silence) Have you ever seen him in this room, Peter?

PETER: No. He's never been here.

ME: Just like he wasn't at your house?

PETER: No. He doesn't come here. He

went to my house. I saw him not be there.

ME: What do you mean, Peter?

PETER: I saw him not be there.

It seems a bit nonsensical to me, and it's that aspect of the account which makes me believe this Man is an imaginary creation. He does not seem to be bound by logic. Let me know if you think I've misheard or misunderstood anything, though.

Kind regards,

Asher

Dr Asher Niazi, Child Psychiatrist

Attached

(1)OpenDownload[PG26.05.17.wav]

Re: P.G. Initial Assessment - CONFIDENTIAL

From: green.em@pattontrust.org

To: asherniazi@nhs.net

Date: 26/05/17

Hi Asher,

Good god, that recording gave me chills. Does he always talk like that? From the transcript I'd imagined confusion, or the uncertainty that Felicity speaks with. But he sounds so…*definite*. As if what he's saying makes complete sense.

I agree with you though–I can't pick out anywhere that you've been mistaken in the transcript. Peter saw a man who wasn't there, but he didn't see him not be somewhere else. It's strange.

I think I may play that recording to Felicity, if I have permission to do so? It may elicit some more details.

Thanks for the file,

Emily

Dr Emily Green, Lead Psychiatrist with The Patton Trust

Re: P.G. Initial Assessment - CONFIDENTIAL

From: asherniazi@nhs.net

To: green.em@pattontrust.org

Date: 26/05/17

Hello Emily,

Yes, you may certainly play the recording to Felicity. I agree that it could bring her to be more descriptive, or at least ascertain whether the children are discussing the same figure.

I'm thinking I'll try to get Peter to draw The Man later this week. It may shed more light on the chance of him being fictional, for example if he has wildly impossible features. Perhaps worth trying with Felicity as well? I know the police tried to get a description from both of them closer to the time, but as we know, they weren't in a state to do so last time it was attempted.

In any case, best of luck,

Asher

Dr Asher Niazi, Child Psychiatrist

Re: P.G. Initial Assessment – CONFIDENTIAL

From: <u>green.em@pattontrust.org</u>

To: <u>asherniazi@nhs.net</u>

Date: 29/05/17

Asher,

My own transcript. Give it a listen. I can't really do it justice. Just read this part, and listen to the file.

PETER (from recording): No. He doesn't come here. He went to my house. I saw him not be there.

ASHER (from recording): What do you –

(EMILY stops the recording)

EMILY: Felicity, is there something you want to tell me? (FELICITY shakes her head) It's just that you reacted when Peter said that. (Silence…23 seconds)

FELICITY: He wasn't there.

EMILY: Who? Who wasn't there? (Silence…35 seconds)

FELICITY: In my bedroom.

EMILY: Pardon? (Silence…5 seconds) Felicity, did you say someone was in your bedroom? (Silence…12 seconds)

FELICITY: Yes. He wasn't there.

EMILY: He was there? Or he wasn't?

FELICITY: Yes.

EMILY: Who? (Silence…6 seconds) Felicity, who are you talking about? (Silence…14 seconds) Felicity? (Silence...11 seconds) Who are—

FELICITY: The Man. He wasn't in my bedroom last night. He said he didn't like you. (Silence…7 seconds)

EMILY: He said he didn't like *you*, or he said he didn't like *me?*

FELICITY: You. He doesn't like questions. He doesn't like you. (Silence - 8 seconds) He didn't like mummy or daddy either.

After that she didn't say a single other thing. Honestly, listen right up to the end of the recording! Not another word for 40 minutes!

I've passed this on to the police as well. No one should have been able to get to her room, she's under lock and key. And no reported break in. So I suppose this backs up the imaginary friend idea? But god, it's sinister.

Emily

Dr Emily Green, Lead Psychiatrist with The

LOCKDOWN PHANTOM #3

Patton Trust

Attached

(1)OpenDownload[FGodwin/29/05/2017.wav]

Re: P.G. Initial Assessment - CONFIDENTIAL

From: asherniazi@nhs.net

To: green.em@pattontrust.org

Date: 01/06/17

Hello Emily,

Sorry, I meant to get back to you sooner, but I've been utterly swamped. Yes, the recording you sent is quite disturbing, but nothing too out of the ordinary. Remember, what seems sinister to adults can be far more innocent in the eyes of a child. I think this discussion of a person in her bedroom, when we know that wasn't the case, is just evidence of this Man figure being fictional. Likely it was something she made up as part of play, a coping mechanism or a dream.

Peter tried drawing The Man yesterday, and the reason I didn't go out of my way to send you details of it before was that it lacked any. Just scribbles, not anything discernible, but when I asked him if it was a good likeness of The Man, Peter said yes. I asked him to identify features (hair colour, skin colour, height etc) and he just said, and I quote, "Like in the picture. That's The Man."

I can send you a scan if you like, but it's hardly worth it. Just scribbles around the edge of the page.

Kind regards,

Asher

Dr Asher Niazi, Child Psychiatrist

Re: P.G. Initial Assessment - CONFIDENTIAL

From: green.em@pattontrust.org

To: asherniazi@nhs.net

Date: 02/06/17

Hi Asher,

Sorry if I was a bit worked up before, it was quite unprofessional of me. You're right, obviously. It's silliness. Make believe.

Felicity's already gone home today–I got more talk of The Man not being there, but nothing as significant as the previous recording–but I'll try getting her to draw him next week.

Thank you for the rational approach, I needed reminding of it. Too many horror films or something I suppose, haha!

Talk to you soon,

Emily

Dr Emily Green, Lead Psychiatrist with The Patton Trust

Re: P.G. Initial Assessment - CONFIDENTIAL

From: asherniazi@nhs.net

To: green.em@pattontrust.org

Date: 02/06/17

Hello Emily,

No problem at all, don't be hard on yourself. You're dealing with traumatised children, possibly ones capable of acts we condition ourselves to believe are only committed by the evil or the insane. It can be a shock to the system; I struggled when I first got into it.

Have a good weekend, try to relax.

Kind regards,

Asher

Dr Asher Niazi, Child Psychiatrist

A. Godwin—illustration - confidential

From: <u>green.em@pattontrust.org</u>
To: <u>asherniazi@nhs.net</u>
Date: 05/06/17

Hi Asher,

I've attached the drawing that Felicity made of The Man—or rather, the drawing she *didn't* make of him! It's bizarre, she spent so long on it, so much care with the strokes of her pencil, I thought she was creating a masterpiece. But all she did was colour in the page black, with a sort of silhouette left in the middle. No details, just blank space—not even a face. I asked her where the details were and she said, "That's what he's like." So I asked why she didn't just do an outline, or just colour in the person-shape in black. She said, "Because he's not there."

I'm definitely in your corner with The Man being some odd bit of imagination now. So what's your conclusion? Do you really think Peter could have done it? Is that what this leaves us with? Do you think he's capable of it?

Emily

Dr Emily Green, Lead Psychiatrist with The Patton Trust

Attached

(1)OpenDownload[FGodwin/05/06/2017.png]

Re: A. Godwin—illustration - confidential

From: asherniazi@nhs.net
To: green.em@pattontrust.org
Date: 06/06/17

Hello Emily,

That caught me by surprise. Felicity's picture is actually startlingly similar to Peter's original. I didn't quite see the silhouette before, because Peter's scribbles are a bit wilder and rougher, but it's definitely there; that gap in the middle is the shape of a man. They seem fixated on this idea of him being, from what I can tell, invisible.

Peter has since made a second image for me, of his own choice. This one is like the other two, but as you can see, the scribbles are a bit angrier, much harsher. He actually ripped through the paper at several points. The silhouette is largely unchanged, except the arms are raised. I asked Peter why he drew this one differently. He said, "Because he's angry, now."

Both drawings attached.

Kind regards,

Asher

Dr Asher Niazi, Child Psychiatrist

Attached (2)OpenDownloadDownload

All[PG31.05.17.jpeg]

[PG06.06.17.jpeg]

Re: A. Godwin—illustration - confidential

From: green.em@pattontrust.org

To: asherniazi@nhs.net

Date: 07/06/17

Hi Asher,

That is really bizarre—Felicity did exactly the same! And I think she referenced you? Not entirely sure, I don't know how she'd know of you, though she probably just presumed that Peter had a psychiatrist since she has one. Here's the transcript:

EMILY: How are you feeling, Felicity? (Silence...12 seconds)

FELICITY: Why?

EMILY: You seem upset. (Silence...25 seconds) Are you upset?

FELICITY: No. (Silence…17 seconds)

EMILY: You've ruined your drawing.

FELICITY: That's what he was like last night.

EMILY: The Man? (Silence…5 seconds) Did you see him? (Silence…19 seconds) Was he there?

FELICITY: No.

EMILY: What happened last night? (Silence…8 seconds)

FELICITY: He's angry with Peter's new friend.

EMILY: Who's Peter's new friend?

FELICITY: Your friend. The one Peter's been talking to.

EMILY: Do you mean—

FELICITY: The Man doesn't like questions. The Man's not happy.

EMILY: Why doesn't The Man—

FELICITY: He wasn't there before. He won't be there now. He won't be at your friend's house tonight. (Silence…7 seconds)

EMILY: I see. (Silence…16 seconds) How…how does that make you feel, Felicity?

FELICITY: Glad.

EMILY: Why glad?

FELICITY: Because I don't like it when he isn't there in my room. And now I won't see him until he's finished.

EMILY: Finished with what? (Silence…23 seconds) Felicity? (Silence…8 seconds) Felicity, until he's finished with what? (Silence…34 seconds) Felicity?

Full audio attached. Any progress with

Peter?

Emily

Dr Emily Green, Lead Psychiatrist with The Patton Trust

Attached

(1)OpenDownload[FGodwin/07/06/2017.wav]

Re: A. Godwin—illustration - confidential

From: green.em@pattontrust.org

To: asherniazi@nhs.net

Date: 08/06/17

Hi Asher,

Did you get my last email? Apologies if you're swamped, just wondering if we're still on for the meeting next week? Tuesday 13th, about 12:30?

Thanks,

Emily

Dr Emily Green, Lead Psychiatrist with The Patton Trust

Everything alright?

From: green.em@pattontrust.org

To: asherniazi@nhs.net

Date: 09/06/17

Hi Asher,

Is everything okay with you? I called your office, they said you've not been in for a few days? We can reschedule the Tuesday meeting, no problem. Let me know if there's anything I can do.

Best wishes,

Emily

Dr Emily Green, Lead Psychiatrist with The Patton Trust

Please reply

From: green.em@pattontrust.org

To: asherniazi@nhs.net

Date: 12/06/17

Asher,

Felicity refused to come in today. The officer stationed at her room says she didn't want to meet The Man. She said he wouldn't be here.

He wouldn't be in my room.

Seriously, Asher, please reply.

Please?

Dr Emily Green, Lead Psychiatrist with The Patton Trust

First published on Reddit.com, 2017

A HARVESTER CALLS

By Johann van der Walt

They had been caught off guard, rendered sympathetic to the plight of a man hurt by nature's violence, and when they opened the door, responding to his constant calls of distress, they found only a nightmare. The dark thing grinned menacingly. Eyes glowing green and a black robe in tatters, as if he had wandered around for centuries.

To their dismay, the fearful realisation of what trickery had transpired caught them completely off guard.

"I have come to collect you, Tom," it said, lifting its arm to reveal a claw opening from a balled fist. "It is time."

Elongated fingers ready to tear through flesh, wriggled and loosened the imprisoned years from its stoned knuckles and limbs, and then it pointed its index finger at the weathered old man.

"How do you know my name?"

"Come with me. Every season must be harvested. There is no bargain to be made," commanded the obsequious cloaked figure. Tom and Martha exchanged a fearful glance.

They were, once of course they understood the gravity of the event, indifferent to his seething instruction.

"Be gone," Tom croaked and slammed the door shut. A valiant and unprecedented move.

A howling wind pushed against the door until the lock gave way and it slammed open once again. This time the Harvester entered.

"All things must come to pass," it offered and reached out to Tom.

The shape yanked him back outside. His stomach bulging forward as if he swallowed a magnet. Suddenly a universal flash of zealous white light illuminated the world, momentarily blinding Martha. She covered her face and fell to the floor. Within seconds, the silence returned. She was alone, with an icy breeze scratching at her cheeks. Tom and the beast were gone.

The seasons must be harvested.

Words she could never forget. That is why she christened him as the Harvester.

What was his purpose? What does it mean to harvest the seasons?

Martha mulled over these questions on many occasions, sinking back into her rocking chair while mourning the loss of the only man she had ever loved.

Another tremor struck. Insidious echoes seeped through the valley. The porcelain in her kitchen cupboard rattled.

He was very close.

Martha made tea and returned to her rocking chair, staring at the front door. Her heart climbed up her throat with trepidation, but she couldn't hide from him. The emptiness was overbearing, and her memory of Tom barely a slither of hope to keep her breathing, was all she had left of humanity. She cocked the shotgun and let it lay against her thigh. Her only chance was to barter with the shape for Tom's return.

Another faint tremor let her cup clatter against the saucer.

Suddenly a deathly silence fell over the world. Minutes to midnight.

"He is here," she gasped softly and placed the cup of tea on the small table next to the chair.

From deep within the woods, she heard trees creak and the ground croak. Silence. Only her heartbeat fired against her eardrums.

***

"Martha...Martha, it's me," pleaded Tom from behind the door.

She sat up straight in surprise, nearly jolting out of her chair. She wanted to believe it.

"Martha, it's freezing."

"Where have you been?"

"Lost. Let me in. Please, Martha."

"Don't underestimate me," she answered in disgust. Her finger caressed the curvature of the trigger. There was only little power in knowing she could possibly hurt this otherworldly thing. What cruel intent did it harbour for using Tom against her? Why did it play such games? From what she had remembered, it could easily tear down the house.

"I have a proposition for you, defiler."

"I'm cold and there are dark things out here," Tom pleaded.

"You are not Tom," she yelled and aimed the shotgun at the door. The hair on the back of her neck stood up.

"You won't fool me again, Harvester. The Winter has claimed my innocence."

A moment of silence followed.

"Harvester?" The dark voice, now having abandoned trickery, mulled over her depiction of it.

A guttural noise rose up, as if from the

ground around the valley. Deep and sinister, it hollowed out into an insidious chuckle.

"Harvester," it repeated. "I have been called many things, but Harvester is by far the most haunting."

"I have a proposition for you, trickster."

"There will be no propositions. The seasons must be harvested. This world is at its end, Martha. A new world is rising."

"What do you mean?"

"The tremors forge new life."

New life? Martha stared at her bony hands, which now looked more like claws. The years had taken their toll on her, mentally and physically, but the sudden feeling of her fragility, radiating off his presence, seeped into her thoughts.

"Bring Tom back," she pleaded, contemplating whether she would be actually able to fire accurately if the opportunity presented itself. She lifted the rifle a few inches. A weapon only for hunting purposes before and deer never fought back.

"Bring him back," she insisted with a little more confidence, clenching her hand tightly around the cold steel barrel.

Still no answer. Suddenly the door swung open. A wave of cold air pierced the interior.

She fired a shot at the threshold—the gaping wound to the outside now empty. The deafening blow thundered through the small cabin, then escaped out into the world, echoing against the pines.

"Bring him back or we both end tonight, I swear it."

"Seasons never return," it scoffed. The voice emanating from somewhere else. Its tone now considerably darker. "This world is dying. How dare you defy me?"

She jumped from her chair and slammed the door shut, just like Tom did so many moons ago. Only this time the rifle was still firmly under one arm, and she kept her eyes on the door and the adjacent window. Where was he?

"We both are monsters tonight," she added softly. Her aged body aching from all the sudden movement. Did he know how weak she was?

"Are we now?"

The Harvester's voice seemed omnipresent, slithering against the walls of every room and vibrating outside amongst the pines. Martha gasped with fear. The shotgun aimed at every possible location where she suspected him to appear.

"What does it mean to harvest seasons?"

Another tremor blasted from underneath the forest. A few trees creaked heavily and fell down, disappearing into the black depths of the vast and lonely world.

"You will see." His voice was somehow even darker and sinister than before, seeping into the house from the top of the roof.

Martha fired a shot against the ceiling,

which sent her crashing into the rocking chair, shotgun spinning across the floor. The door swung open, and the Harvester moved past the threshold but didn't enter yet. They exchanged glances. His green eyes penetrating her thoughts. Fear froze her cold.

"Why are you doing this? Where did you take Tom?"

"Winter collects what it's due. Seasons come and go." He disappeared fluidly.

"No," she returned boldly, even surprising herself. "I am no season, nor am I something to collect. You bring death to my door, and I refuse to accept it."

A silence followed. Martha swore she heard a heavy sigh. Did the Harvester consider her proposal? Was she finally getting through to him? Did this mean that she could bargain a deal? Martha shook the frozen state to the extent that she could muster up enough strength and head to the opposite side of the room to collect the rifle and shut the door once again. It moved like a shadow, carving horizontal trenches into the walls outside as his claws ran along the wooden exterior. Her own heartbeat so loud that she could hear it bounce off the walls.

An unfamiliar shriek infused the landscape with a thunderous blow, and another tremor followed. It cracked the wooden floor underneath her. She let go of the rifle, yielding to the overwhelming elements. It would be of no use to her. Who was that? Surely not the beast waiting to pounce?

A succession of smaller intense tremors hit the cabin, and she staggered backwards, stumbling onto the floor. Her ankle popped and she cried out in pain, cowering in the foetal position. Some invisible force punched her in the stomach, and she scolded, "Have you not destroyed enough? My home? My love? What have I done to you? Why do I deserve this?"

"How long was the summer, Martha?"

"What?"

More scratches against the house. Muffled voices followed. Voices that did not originate from him, or anyone else for that matter.

Suddenly his voice projected from the kitchen behind her, and she swung her body around.

"You seem to forget that it has long been since you felt the cold."

"The summer," she gasped. It dawned on her, amidst her fear and confusion. The summer had indeed been reigning over the valley ever since Tom's disappearance. How did she not remember the change in the seasons? Almost a week after Tom's disappearance, the summer had returned almost immediately, melting all the snow within a week. Ever since then it had been summer up until the change of the season two weeks ago. Gradually at first, but the last week had seen the return of the storms and intense earthquakes.

She tried to stand up and felt a fresh wave of pain shoot through her ankle. She bit her lip and kicked maniacally.

Another tremor blasted up from earth's core. She could feel the vibrations under the cabin's foundation. She felt an uncanny connection to the tremor, as if it had somehow erupted because of her existence.

"What does it mean? What does this all mean?"

He leapt into the sky and landed on the roof with a loud thud. More dust sprinkled on the floor.

"From the old worlds, new ones are forged. Do you not understand, Martha? Do you not feel this world's decay? There is nothing for you here."

Martha shrieked. A headache pounded at her temples, and again the knowledge of her fleeting mortality flickered like warning signs in her thoughts. The end of this world, the passing of old things, reverberated through her body. The only thing that she had left was life. Life. The commodity he wanted to take from her.

"What are you?"

"Ancient. The gatekeeper between worlds."

More muffled voices, ineligible and yet so close she swore they were inside the house.

"Why did you kill Tom?" She rose to her feet. The pain shot through her body, but she wasn't going to die a coward.

"He is not dead."

"What?"

Pearls of sweat, even with the ensuing

cold wind, formed on her forehead. Her heart so loud now she struggled to hear her own thoughts.

"Where is Tom?"

The revelation almost knocked her wind out and blood drained from her head, sending her tumbling to the floor. "His name is not Tom anymore. He doesn't remember you."

The Harvester broke the front door off its hinges and tossed it into the dark. He stepped into frame and wriggled his elongated fingers, shaking snow and wet dust, the dead skin of this world, from his hands.

"He now lives in a world forged from this decaying world. Did he not complain about the winter, Martha? How it killed everything? Think. Back when the tremors started."

He was right. She recalled such a conversation. Tom told her that the world looked somehow different, and that he seemed to struggle to hear the trees whistle and birds sing as he did before.

It was information overload. Martha couldn't deal with it. Her confusion disoriented her completely.

"You took everything from me," she cried, struggling to inhale as cold air choked her. The sight of the figure sent shivers down her spine. The surrounding darkness, a void—somehow worse than the night outside—and the green glowing eyes, all products of constant nightmares.

"How can you be so cruel?"

From behind the cloaked figure she saw lights wash up from deep within the forest, swallowing the world along the way.

"This is the end of the road, Martha."

"No," she protested. Tears burnt cold tracks down her cheeks. She crawled into the kitchen. Another earthquake struck and shattered all the windows around the house.

Again she felt the intense sensation in her stomach, like an abrupt tug, trying to yank her out of her body.

"I have come to harvest you," said the dark voice.

Outside the kitchen she heard muffled screams. Was it real?

"What is happening to me?"

The Harvester raised his hand and

pulled an invisible lasso, reeling her from out the kitchen back into the lounge. The fire in the fireplace had finally died. Orange glowing coals now fading.

"What is happening?"

"The old world is dying."

He opened his palm and as if the grip from the rope had been released; she inhaled deeply. The pressure on her stomach dissipated.

Blinding white lights closed in on them.

"Time to go, Martha."

"No," she whispered in final protest, weathered beyond physical reserve.

"Let's go," it commanded and grabbed her mercilessly, wrapping its long fingers around her throat. The earth shook, ready to deliver its greatest tremor yet, and they moved towards the door frame. She started coughing uncontrollably. Fluid escaped her lungs. Pain coursed through her entire body. The lights swallowed both of them. She felt someone tugging at her stomach, the 'n sharp noise, and then the pressure was relieved.

"You bring death," she said. It sounded like an echo instead of a solid voice.

"No," it answered back, also an echo. "I bring life."

Outside a brilliant whiteness shot up into the sky, colouring the entire world and blinding everything in sight. She stuck out her arms, childishly trying to hold on to something. Martha felt his grip loosen and inhaled. Never before, even without Tom around, did she feel this level of loneliness. The air cut down her throat and burned red hot in her chest. She started crying. Giant hands pulled and tugged on her, and she exchanged hands from one giant to another. The muffled voices rose up again, this time more vivid, much closer.

Around her, the temperature dropped, and then suddenly she was wrapped in something.

All her memories from the forest dissipated with every passing second as her eyes slowly scouted this new world she was in. She found comfort and warmth close to someone. Another heartbeat close to her ear.

Incredible warmth oozed from this

stranger who now cradled her. Martha felt loved. No more entrenching melancholy and isolation.

***

Far away, in a distant realm, a lone creature walked deep into the forest, heading to an isolated cabin. Tremors shook the landscape. For the inhabitants of the small wooden house deep in the valley, another world had already been forged. He was only the gatekeeper between worlds. Death forges life, and so the cycle continues. The Harvester collects only what is due.

The beginning of the end is the beginning of everything.

CIRCLES OUT OF SALT

By J. Agombar

The room was dimly lit by a handful of thick cream candles scattered around, burning a sweet lemongrass scent. The walls were draped with crimson curtains and the window had been covered with black sugar paper. A large, rectangular oak table stood central; the wood much lighter than that of the creaky floorboards. The old man's hands trembled as he shook salt out from the bag. Dragging it out around the table, he stumbled over a chair leg, scattering some over the seat and his warped brown leather boots. The heavy door creaked open behind him, and from the darkness of the chancel came a man of no more than twenty-five with a tall, slim build; a man he knew well.

"Gerry! Thank God I've found you! What are you doing here?" he said, slightly out of breath and leaving the door open behind him.

"I told you not to come here tonight,

Anthony, you know how this works," the old man grumbled.

Anthony Simm walked toward him with a pained expression. He recognised Gerry mostly from his attire these days—red chequered shirt with blue cargo trousers, and those worn-out boots. Those were the same clothes he remembered him by from ten years ago, when things were normal. His change of mannerisms and faded features were what crushed him, along with the greyish beard, the weathered hands, and the bags under his eyes. This was how he couldn't bear to see Gerry.

"It's mum, she's been taken ill. She's asking to speak to you from the hospital," Anthony said.

The old man stopped and met his gaze

in shock for just a moment. He blinked and then changed expression.

"I'm disappointed, Anthony. You never were a good liar, but I didn't think you'd ever be using your mother as an excuse."

Anthony closed his eyes and rubbed the back of his head in despair over the truth the old man spoke. "I…I get it. She's fine, but I…I knew you wouldn't buy anything else. You won't stop doing this every year for anybody now."

The old man ignored him and continued salting around the table.

"You know, that was the first time I recall you looking at me in the eye for years. That's what it takes for you these days," Anthony pushed.

"I'm doing it for your father, boy!" the old man said as he completed the circle of salt. "I understand if nobody else in the family wants to help, which is why I don't ask."

"It's not going to bring him back, Gerry!"

The old man ignored him again and picked up a sturdy broom that leant against the wall and walked toward the door behind Anthony. Anthony blocked the way by spreading his arms and they paused in front of each other.

"I'm an old man, Anthony. I can't overpower you, but if I don't do it here in this sacred place, then I'll just end up somewhere else in secret next year."

Anthony tried hard to stop his eyes

from welling up.

"I have to know who it was who killed him," Gerry stated.

"It was seven years ago! We should just let it lie!"

Gerry frowned and glared at him, disapprovingly.

"As far as I know, we *have* let it lie, for seven years! He was my brother, and *your* father!" Gerry went red and started to spit through his teeth a little. Realising his outburst, he retracted his anger. "I'm sorry. But I can't let it go. If I live another twenty years, I'll still be doing it."

Anthony breathed heavily as a tear rushed down his cheek. He lowered his arm and scanned the arched ceiling in search for distraction.

"How do you know this voodoo shit won't end up being the death of you too?" he asked.

Gerry looked him in the eye once more and placed a hand on his shoulder.

"If it ends that way, then at least I can ask him myself."

Anthony responded by slamming the door behind him on the way out, breaking the circle of salt with his Nike trainers as he left.

***

Canewdon church was rarely visited in the isolated village of the same name, yet dubbed as one of the most haunted churches in the whole of England. Each year since the 1980s it had grown in popularity, especially on Halloween, where the police now had to tape it off to the public. Pagans and White Witches had flocked in the last two decades, chanting rituals and drinking from plastic moulded skulls. The whole affair had become a ludicrous pantomime where even drunken teenagers ended up joining in to impress their friends. However, much stranger events had been reported over the years, including a rabbit infestation that disappeared overnight, a phantom horse that ran wild through the nearby creek, a crusader knight seen patrolling the local streets, and more commonly, a faceless woman in a poke bonnet who roamed the grounds before descending to the river and crossing it as if floating. The latter had been reported during the night and the daylight.

None of this had interested Gerard Simm until recent years, where he had turned to the contacts of 'Wicca' for solace. He was friends with the sexton of the church who allowed him a key to perform these occasional gatherings, and on the basis that the church was left the way it was found with no disturbances to the area.

Anthony raised his hood as he crossed the car park to prevent his hair from soaking further in the rain that came down hard. It dashed off the windscreen as he stepped into his Citroen C3. He fumbled for the key and started the engine. The streaming tears fell from his face onto his lap as he flicked the windscreen wipers on full swing. With tense hands upon the wheel, he started to shake and convulse with desperate upset, but knew that he had to get a hold of himself before driving home. A part of him became fearful for leaving. The thought of his uncle sitting in that strange church with a group of strangers unnerved him. Was it worse to stay and wait? He wasn't sure. He shook his head whilst toying with the idea for a moment, but eventually flicked on the headlights. He then noticed something upon the grass at the edge of the car park; a greyish rabbit sat staring at him, upright and still. For a moment he thought it may be an ornament until it snapped its head in the direction of the gate. Anthony was startled by two shafts of light that passed over him, causing him to squint. Another small hatchback entered the car park and pulled up about twenty feet away. A female figure stepped out and started towards the church. She carried a rucksack that looked heavy. He glanced back towards the beams of his own headlights to find the rabbit was gone. He ground his teeth for a moment before smacking the wheel twice with his right hand. Fumbling through the neck of his t-shirt, he grabbed hold of a pendant that hung around his neck and squeezed his eyes shut in prayer.

"I'm sorry it had to come to this, dad," he voiced.

He flicked the engine off, stepped out of the car, and walked back over to the church.

***

As he stood in the old building, the

grey walls felt like they imprisoned him. Moving toward the large arched door he heard the conversation between his uncle and the woman become clearer. He entered the room slowly and found both of them staring.

"Hello, young man," said the woman. "Are you another who will be joining the session tonight?"

Anthony, hair still dripping wet, eyed his uncle, who answered for him, anxiously.

"Maria. This is Anthony, my nephew. I'm not sure he would want to join us. His father is the purpose of tonight."

"Oh, I see. I'm sorry to hear of your loss, Anthony," Maria replied.

"I guess you're the voodoo woman

who is conducting tonight's gathering?" he replied, raising an eyebrow.

"*Medium.* I'm known as a *medium.* And yes, I conduct the *seance*, young man," she replied, smiling. "And pleased to meet you too. Feel free to join us if you wish, but I understand if this is hard for you."

Anthony's eyebrows twitched from irritation before he removed his coat and hung it upon the rack on the wall. He took the nearest seat and swept his sodden hair behind his ears before taking a few deep breaths with hands wrapped around the back of his neck.

Gerry and Maria glanced at each other, signalling the strain of the situation.

"Feel free to set up, Maria. Two more

should be here shortly. One more won't hurt, will it?" Gerry asked.

"Of course not. Five actually works better for the contact. One for each arm of the pentagram."

As she spoke, she revealed from her bag a large metal contraption; circular, sturdy, and placed it flat upon the table. Its base was a pentagram scored as grooves into a metallic plate. Inset between the grooves were three candle holders, which she filled with three red scented candles and lit them. Around the outer edge of the pentagram was a raised circular plate with mottled and embossed metal. Scored into this was each letter of the alphabet and numbers zero to nine. The plate could be rotated and highlighted letters through a hole in a planchette fixed to one side. Anthony looked beguiled by the object for a moment, but then shifted his gaze to glance further at the medium. She was around early forties in a purple singlet top. Her shoulders were covered by a black cardigan with a striking red floral design. Her light brown bobbed hair hung past her thin face toward an extravagant necklace. Bangles and beads of cerulean and ruby huddled around a silver crescent moon. Anthony was then distracted by footsteps and voices from the main part of the church. The heavy door creaked open once more, assisted by the medium, and two more women walked through.

One woman, large and outspoken, was clearly a friend of Gerry. She hugged him and introduced herself in a jovial way around the table. The way she greeted the medium suggested they had also met before. Her friend walked in behind her, a skinnier, more reserved woman with a gaunt face. She wore a somewhat colourless dress under a brown rain-mac and smiled subtly, like the Mona Lisa, with palms overlapped modestly. They both stepped into the now very segmented circle of salt and took a seat.

"Are all these people necessary?" Anthony asked.

"They are all willing, trusted people, Anthony," Gerry replied.

"What's with all the salt everywhere?"

"It's a barrier to stop unwanted spirits interfering," Maria answered.

Anthony raised one eyebrow.

The large woman was introduced as Cara, and Elise was her friend who walked in with her. Anthony had little interest in who they were, but Cara claimed to have known his father. Maria asked everybody to remove their jewellery before starting the session and place it on a small stool in the corner. A watch and several bracelets and necklaces were removed, but Anthony decided to ignore the request and hide his etched gold pendant under the neckline of his t-shirt. They each took their seats once again to begin as Maria used the broom to re-establish the circle of salt. As Maria returned to her seat, Anthony dragged his leg back a little behind his chair and scraped the barrier of salt with his sole. He coughed a little to cover the sound.

"Thank you all for coming. We are all here tonight to find details of the death of Richard Simm. Present are a mixture of friends and family who would like to contact the spirits tonight in an attempt to find his killer," Maria confirmed.

Maria gestured to Gerry who then reached into his satchel on the floor and pulled from it a portrait photograph of his brother. It seemed like one of his wedding photos from what he wore; a smart suit with a blue tie.

Anthony stared at his father's picture for a moment and forced himself to glance away.

Maria encouraged each of them to join hands, forming a circle around the table.

She closed her eyes and started to regulate her breathing to a slow and steady rhythm. She then advised each of them to do the same and that contact was about to be made.

Anthony felt it was too late to not play along, but his eye twitched open occasionally in the silence. He frowned at how serious Gerry looked. His suspicions that his uncle was infatuated with these unhinged events were now confirmed.

"Spirits. Nether. Beyond. We invite you to join us in our task. We seek answers simply to benefit the deceased, the victims, and so that the offender may be brought to justice in this world. Firstly, we call upon Richard Simm. Richard, please signal to us that you are here and willing to provide answers…," said Maria.

A moment of silence passed and the rain outside seemed to ease. Everyone opened their eyes and the air in the room became deathly still. Suddenly, a candle flickered, and everyone fixed their eyes upon it, wondering if it was actually a sign. Maria also seemed to be unsure, but attempted to clarify.

"Richard, if you are present, we would like to ask you who your murderer was. Can you name him? Can you identify him?" she asked.

Another moment of unnerving silence lingered. Maria persisted in her inquiry.

"Richard Simm. Are you able to—"

Suddenly, she was interrupted by a gasp from everyone, startled at the sound of a phone going off in the room. A hideous pop song served as the ringtone which came from the pocket of one of the coats hung on the wall by the door. Cara placed one hand across her chest in shock whilst Gerry clenched his fists upon the table. Elise seemed to be the only one to not react beyond breaking the circle of hands. Anthony expressed a mixture of embarrassment and fright, but was the first to stand and fetch his phone.

"Sorry. That would be mine," he said, fumbling for the phone and taking it out of the room to answer it.

The medium shook her head and glanced at Gerry, who rubbed the back of his own head with both hands. Their eyes met with mutual irritation before Anthony returned to the room. His expression was different now, the colour had drained from his face a little and he blinked anxiously.

"Was it someone important?" asked Gerry.

"Just a strange voice. I think it was a wrong number, maybe. I'm sorry. I've turned it off now. Shall we continue?" Anthony replied, returning the phone to the jacket pocket.

Maria checked with everyone else about their phones before seeing Anthony collect the broom from behind her and sweep the salt back into a neat circle. He then took his seat.

Maria took a moment to retrieve more items from her bag. She placed another object on the table; a small crystal cut-glass bowl. She then poured bottled water in, almost filling it. She then placed an A3 page of black sugar paper behind the bowl of water and poured a small pile of ground chalk onto it.

"Let's try something different," she said.

The group re-joined their hands and took long, deep breaths to regain composure.

"Spirits of Canewdon. Tonight, we wish to gain information surrounding the death of Richard Simm. We summon the spirit of Rose Pye to speak on his behalf. She is known to still be present in these parts and has been spotted around the fields and trees nearby. Although she was known to use various names to disguise herself,

Rose was believed to peacefully practise the powers of Wicca in this region and was unjustly left to perish under lock and key, despite being acquitted of the crime of which she was accused. We ask you tonight to show your presence in hope to reveal the aggressor of another unjust murder," Maria voiced, thoughtfully.

Another moment passed as the room fell silent again but gradually, subtly, the room darkened as the candles scattered around the room slowly went out, leaving only the three red ones on the table flickering. As it became dim enough to not see the surroundings outside the circle, the bowl of water moved. It tilted to one side as if gravity was shifting, causing a little to spill onto the black paper below. Maria's eyes widened.

"I can feel your presence. We welcome you and appreciate the chance to communicate. Are you able to answer our questions?" Maria asked.

A creak came from the contraption in front of them. The rotating metal plate moved slowly around the device on the table about an inch across so that the planchette windowed the word 'YES' which was scored into the metal as a full word next to the blank starting point. The word 'NO' was scored the other side of it for clarity.

The attendees breathed deeply. Cara and Elise seemed fixed with elation, whereas Anthony and Gerry contained an anxious ambivalence. Maria breathed deeper out of relief and became more assertive from this contact.

"We thank you, Rose Pye. Can you tell us, is the soul of Richard Simm willing to speak to us?" Maria asked.

The plate on the device moved again, slowly, but in the opposite direction. It stopped, displaying: 'NO'.

"What? Why is that? Tell him his brother and son are here!" Gerry demanded.

Maria attempted to console Gerry by rubbing the hand she already held and asked him to trust her skills. When he relented, she closed her eyes and continued.

"Spirit. If he is not contented, we would like to know why," she stated.

The dial in front stood still for another moment, and the medium felt Anthony's grip tighten on her hand. Then, suddenly, the plate moved again, clockwise, then anticlockwise in varying order. It spelt the letters 'P.A.I.N.F.U.L'.

Gerry watched each letter with guilt, but then saw with sorrow that Anthony had closed his eyes tight and released a tear that rolled down one side of his face.

"Why is his pain still strong?" Maria asked.

The dial started to move again, but slower, as if trying to crack the code of a safe. The letters spelt out slowly, 'K.I.L.L.E.R.I.S.H.E.R'.

Gerry frowned and whispered the words as they formed. His eyes widened and darted around at all three women at the table as the dial slowed to almost a halt, but it continued to move before landing on the final letter, 'E'.

"Here! Surely it can't be true! There must be some mistake!" Gerry exclaimed, now glancing at each of them as the scope of accusation widened.

Anthony developed a neurotic scowl. His grip tightened so much that Maria was forced to prize his hand from her own.

"How can you be so sure this is truth, Maria? Tell us, is this not a mistake, somehow?" asked Cara, thoughtfully.

"This is very unusual, but I can still feel that the connection is pure and free of the uninvited. The spirits have no reason to lie, unless…" Maria explained.

"Unless what?" asked Gerry.

"Unless the words are ambiguous. 'Killer is here' could mean that the killer is already dead. It is the spirit world who is speaking through Rose Pye. The killer may be amongst *them*."

Cara glanced around at the group and lingered on Elise a little more than she meant to before shaking her head solemnly at the device on the table. "If that is the case, how do we continue this now?"

"Easily," Gerry cut in. "Whoever did it won't want to follow it through. If they are seated here, then they will be outed. If they are seated in the spirit world, then surely we can find out more. So I say we should ask more of the Wicca woman."

Maria blinked, trying not to glance at

anybody around her. She pursed her lips in thought before offering another solution.

"If required, I can establish contact privately before proceeding. Ask some questions to see what the spirits say to me before I relay it," she suggested.

"How can you do that? I thought you said you needed the energy of all of us to make a connection?" Anthony asked.

"I don't require everybody, but it helps. I will need your hands again. However, I can tap in completely on my own. It's like I have a phone line in my head that only I can control. I can see who picks up, but if I am surrounded by a group of associated people, it narrows the possibility of who picks up. I now have Rose Pye on line one, so to speak. I don't usually offer it as it can be exhausting for me, but under the circumstances it may help. I can't guarantee it will be good news though."

Each of the guests took a pensive expression as she continued.

"There is one issue. Sometimes the call can transfer—this is when the spirit takes possession and speaks through somebody else, and you won't have control."

The foreboding around the table weighed heavily upon each of them to hear such a premise. But when Maria asked them one by one if they were ready to take the risk, they each nodded, including Anthony, who stared glassy eyed at his dad's wedding photo. As they all joined hands again Maria closed her eyes and tapped into the spirit world once more. The curtains in the corner swayed gently from a subtle breeze, and the candles that had been starved earlier had created a smoke that distorted the ceiling above them. Everyone else kept their eyes open and unblinking.

"Rose Pye. If the killer is amongst us at this table, please tell me alone. If they are with you in the spirit world, please show us a sign," Maria voiced.

At that moment nothing changed but Maria's expression. All of them paid close attention to her frowning and cocking her head to one side. Anthony noticed her move as if struggling to hear something, but then her cheeks relaxed, and her mouth gaped slightly. Her breathing seemed to stop entirely; her body halted from moving as if frozen. He then noticed his uncle Gerry and Cara freeze in the same way. In front of the medium, the powdered chalk started to move and skip across the paper as if being spread by an invisible hand. A strange feeling ran through Anthony as he held the hands of the frozen medium and, on the other side, Elise, who was not frozen, but stared at him intensely. Anthony swallowed hard.

"What's happening?" he asked, unsure if she would know. He could detect something wasn't right.

"You should not have come here, boy!" spat Elise.

Anthony recoiled and tried to pull his hand away but couldn't. Her grip became unnaturally strong. Her voice was different, lower, piercing in tone and full of spite. Fear struck him as he recognised it.

"The sun will burn! You will repent! You disgust me!" she snarled.

Spittle flew from Elise's mouth as she snarled, but he was certain that the speaker was not Elise. The words chilled him to his core as he also recognised them, the same words he had heard through the phone earlier. He cowered and thrashed to release his arm. A moment of terror caused him to convulse, but eventually he managed to snatch it away from her grip. But as soon as he did, whatever took hold of Elise faded as she flickered her eyes and placed her hands calmly upon the table. She looked drained and held her throat in pain.

The others suddenly regained movement and calmly let go of each other. They seemed disorientated as the candlelight increased.

"What did you hear?" Gerry asked the medium.

"Strange. The connection lapsed, but I did hear somethi—"

Anthony interrupted her as he screamed in pain, clasping his neck. He wrestled with what at first appeared to be an invisible pair of hands clutching him, but it quickly became clear he was trying to remove something from underneath his t-shirt. He ripped from his neck his gold pendant and tossed it across the table. It landed in the bowl of water, steaming and revealing the etched symbol of a sun with flailing arms. Circular burns were left upon his chest and scorched parts of his hands and neck where the chain had rubbed. He was left panting, eyes streaming. He glanced at Elise briefly before covering his face with his hands.

"Enough! It was me. It was an accident. But I killed my father," he choked through his tears.

All at the table seemed confused and had no memory of Elise's possession. They failed to see what had caused Anthony to confess. The medium spoke first as she noticed the chalk in front of her spread out on the sugar paper in the shape of a burning sun with flailing flares.

Maria had established the spirit of Rose Pye had transferred through them to

Elise. She claimed the events that only Anthony could witness were due to an anger within the Wicca spirit, and admitting that the killer being present in the room could have resulted in a much worse consequence if a confession was not made. Anthony stayed in the room, explaining all he could to Gerry whilst the others gathered their belongings.

A while later the medium packed her items away and said goodbye to Gerry by the main entrance, saying that payment for her services was not to be settled tonight, but another night when tensions had died down. Elise was next to leave and wished Gerry and Anthony peace. Gerry thanked her and shook her hand before she walked away into the darkness of the car park. Cara came to the door a little less vocal than usual and stifled her yawning.

"I'm so sorry to hear all these revelations, Gerry. Are you going to be alright?" she asked.

"I'll be fine. It's *him* I'm worried about," he said, gesturing inside to Anthony. "We'll have to figure out where to go from here. His mother will be devastated."

Cara nodded sheepishly. "Oh, lord. If there's anything I can do, please let me know," she kissed Gerry on the cheek. "Oh, I meant to ask, what was wrong with that pendant?"

"It was a gift from his father on his eighteenth. Possibly the last gift he received. He's always worn it. It's an item that connects them. He killed him in a rage during an argument; blunt object impact. The police never found the culprit as the front door was left open. They assumed it was a disturbed burglar. Turns out Anthony had just ran off. It explains why Richard wouldn't appear to say what happened. I wonder if it means that he's forgiven him."

"Do you forgive him?" she asked.

"I have no idea yet," he replied.

Gerry lit a cigarette and put it to his mouth.

"I thought you gave up," Cara said.

"I did. I just started again now," he pondered in thought as he glanced across the darkness of the car park. "Aren't you giving your friend a lift home?"

"My friend? You mean Elise? Oh, no,

we only met just tonight. She seemed nice."

Gerry raised one eyebrow in confusion.

"I thought she was the friend you were bringing with you tonight?"

"No. Claire couldn't get a babysitter, so I came alone. I thought she was a friend of *yours*."

The cigarette hung loosely from his gaping mouth as Gerry squinted toward the darkness of the car park and the fields behind. The only movement he could make out was the figure of a rabbit silhouetted in the moonlight, hopping away towards the treeline in the distance.

First published in Crimes & Apparitions, Michael Terrence publishing, 2018

HUNTING SHADOWS

By Alannah K. Pearson

The wild fury that had consumed me faded to a whispered breeze. I felt lost, confused and incredibly weary. I looked about myself, noticing the solemn bulk of the church that stood in the centre of the city. Autumn leaves tumbled slowly about me, twisting in their dive toward the pavement. I stared down at my bare feet, memories stirring through the haze of confusion. I glanced up again at the sandstone church opposite me, half-hidden by the shadows from the taller modern skyscrapers surrounding it. Around me, the usually busy streets in the centre of the city were empty. The wrongness was jarring.

What had happened to me? Where was Nick? I tried to recall the past few days, but there was only a hollow where my life should have been. Memory stirred sluggishly, that final argument with Nick. The reproachful glare he had given me and the sound of the book he was reading as it hit and floor with a loud thwack! I had ignored his concerns and promises of love. Instead, I'd kicked the book before stalking from the room, *Biblical Folklore* spinning drunkenly across the floor to hit the opposite wall. I'd left the house and never returned.

I shivered, trying to forget the darkness that had consumed me then, suffocating as it was inescapable. But there were no more memories or emotions after I'd left Nick, I could dredge nothing more from my mind. Frowning, I stared at the autumn leaves in the gutter. A sudden, wrenching terror woke in me. It had been early autumn when I'd left the house, and the leaves were only beginning to turn gold. *How long had I been gone?*

Broken glass glittered beneath an

overhead light and caught my attention. I stared at the dark shadows where overgrown hedges lined a narrow passage. A huge dog moved through the shadows in the churchyard, its bulk disguised only as a darker shade of night. I heard a distant but familiar voice and turned quickly away from the hound.

A little further down the street to my right, on the fringe of flashing emergency vehicles, Nick stared numbly at the red and blue lights refracting off the wet city street. He stood, hands shoved deep into his overcoat pockets, head lowered, shoulders hunched against the cold. A few meters away, a body lay against the dark brick wall, water leaking from the overhead gutter pooling around it, a blue crime scene tarp secured over the unmoving form.

I moved closer to Nick, only a few meters from him now, but he remained unresponsive, not flinching or startling at my sudden appearance. Perhaps he couldn't see me—none of the police officers seemed to react to me. Worried but I still unsure, I drew closer again. Nick still did not respond, seeming deep within himself. I continued to approach but stopped, right behind his shoulder now, his hollow eyes never shifting from the ground.

"Nick?" I asked, my breath brushing his cheek, but he didn't respond to my voice.

I looked around us, noticing no one had responded to my voice. I glanced down at my bare feet again, a terrible suspicion growing stronger within me. Something was very wrong with me.

"Nick!" I called, pushing energy into my voice, stirring a breeze along the pavement, autumn leaves skittering into the gutter.

Nick frowned at the leaves until they stopped moving and then sighed, gaze lifting briefly to the body near the alley wall, before he lowered his eyes again.

I had been desperate to find Nick. He had been the only one who cherished me in life, the one who really saw me. It seemed cruel that now I was as absent to him as if I had never existed. Anger burned in me. I poured that rage into whatever strength I possessed and stared at Nick's solemn profile, my gaze boring into him, willing him to turn his head and *see* me. Nothing. Determined to somehow make Nick see, I drew the energy I had inside myself, summoning it like a breath waiting to be exhaled. The atmosphere around us grew tense and crackled, my form wavering slightly with the shifting breeze.

"Nick," I growled, bare branches of the tree above his head rattling together.

"Don't go using yourself up too fast like that, girl," an old man said suddenly, breaking my concentration.

I turned in wonder. I hadn't heard him approach but now stood, a wizened figure in his faded clothing, grey beard and unkempt hair. His features were kindly, face weathered from a lifetime of experience and most of it hard.

"*You* can see me," I said, shocked.

"Of course," the old man replied, grinning to reveal a few missing teeth. "Shouldn't I?"

"Well, it's just no one has been able to see me until now," I explained, indicating Nick who was completely unaware of me.

The old man nodded sagely and gestured to me to approach him where he waited a few paces from the alley. I glanced at Nick who remained oblivious before walking over to the old man, his unruly grey eyebrows knitted in concern.

"You've not been with us long, have you, girl?" the old man asked. "Us?" I asked, dreading the answer I already knew.

"The dearly departed," he explained, kind eyes regarding me. "You're a ghost."

"Then you're a ghost too," I said, deflated.

"Don't look so crestfallen," the old man replied. "You're not alone any longer, girl."

"I wasn't alone," I said defensively.

"Oh?" he asked, stepping away from me a little. "Never mind, then."

"When I was alive," I added hurriedly, not wanting him to leave. "I'm alone now."

"That's not entirely true," he replied, kindly. "That man don't come here for the living."

I frowned, following his gaze. "Nick?" I asked in surprise.

"He's been coming here for a month

now. He ain't looking for a living person."

"He's looking for me," I began. "I remember a creature of shadows," I said slowly, memory returning in awful detail. "It fed on me until there was nothing left but flesh. It convinced me I was alone, that there was nothing but hopelessness and pain. It *lied* to me," I finished, meeting the old man's gaze.

The old man nodded, pausing in his task of picking through a stack of discarded crates at the alley mouth while I talked.

"Do you know about the demon?" I asked, saying the last word uncertainly, but it seemed the right term for it. I glanced to Nick, half-expecting him to correct me with his usual library of obscure knowledge of folklore and mythology. But he didn't correct me, instead he'd moved a few steps away to speak with one of the approaching officers.

"Most of us know about the demon," the old man answered, not even glancing at me from his task sorting through cans and discarded treasure from other people's lives. "We all know to stay away from it. You'd be wise to do the same, girl."

"Wisdom isn't exactly what I've been known for," I muttered.

The man only grunted in agreement, moving to the next dumpster with a resigned sigh.

"I need to make amends," I explained. "That man standing there is the only one who can warn others. Tell me what you know about the demon so I can stop it," I pleaded.

"I know you can't destroy something like that," the man replied. "Neither can your friend, no matter what kind of good person he might be. There are some beings in this world that are immune to death. That demon is one of them."

I stared at the wall opposite me, a scrawl of incomprehensible graffiti and a half-obscured mural of the park. I recognised a stylised version of the statue of Queen Victoria and, half-hidden in the depths of the garden foliage, familiar red eyes stared from the hulking form of a black dog.

"What about that dog then?" I asked, looking up at the old man in excitement. "The black dog. Is it some sort of hell hound that follows the demon? Or does it hunt it?"

"Ah!" the old man said with an appreciative whistle. "Now you might have some mighty harebrained plan there, but it won't work. That dog isn't with the demon, but it can't be commanded either."

"Then what is it?" I asked, becoming increasingly frustrated.

"You know the black dog from all those stories people speak about? The ones with the depression?" he asked, the way he called it 'the depression' made me think he predated the term. I gave a quick nod anyway, and he grinned happily. "Well, old Winston Churchill wasn't wrong about the depression being like having your own black dog. That demon causes sorrow when it feeds, as you well know, girl. Now the dog seems to track that sorrow, like a scent, always hunting the demon. No one alive nor dead knows what the dog will do if it catches the demon since no one thinks that's ever happened before."

"Can the dog destroy the demon, then?" I asked.

He shrugged his bony shoulders. "Don't know if it can or not. Seems the dog just chases the demon off again," he agreed. "But if you're really determined to go hunting this demon, get yourself a good tracking dog to do it with."

"You think the dog will help me?" I asked, incredulously.

"I think that dog wants the same quarry you do. He might catch it if he had some help."

I smiled, grabbing the old man in a quick but fierce hug. He rattled an uncomfortable chuckle, patting me awkwardly on the back and embarrassed, shied away from my gratitude.

"Now, now," he said, still chuckling. "Go find that dog and tell your friend what to do," he said. "And don't expend too much of that energy either. You poltergeists run hot, and it don't last forever," he warned.

"Thank you," I replied, watching as he gave a little wave and disappeared around the corner at the end of the street.

I hesitated, thinking about what he'd just told me. The demon caused a sorrow that the hound could track; I wondered if these frequent storms we'd had lately were like a track made by the hound? If they were, maybe I could follow the erratic thunderstorms to find the hound and that way, the demon too. I returned my attention to Nick, who had finished speaking to the police officer. They were now shaking hands—the unmarked morgue vehicle had silently arrived, and officers were already opening the back doors.

"We appreciate you keeping an eye on these kids," the officer was saying to Nick, his expression openly concerned. "But it won't bring Alisha back. Are you getting any counselling?"

Nick's lips only tightened into a thin but determined smile that instantly worried me. "I appreciate your concern, but I'm managing okay," he lied and stepped away, a sidelong glance at the unmarked van.

The careless disregard for his own well-being was so uncharacteristic of Nick that I was momentarily stunned. I stood motionless, watching him walk away from the alley, shoulders still hunched against the burden he carried. I ignored the warning I'd just been given by the ghost of the old homeless man. I needed Nick to see me now, beyond anything else, he needed to know I hadn't left him.

"Nick!" I shouted, voice urgent as I hurried after him, my hand grasping his shoulder.

He flinched and stepped away from me, eyes wide as he half-spun, staring at the emptiness before him. He could *feel* me but could not *see* me. I lifted my hand, reaching to touch him again, but stopped at a sudden movement on the periphery of my vision.

On the opposite street corner, the massive bulk of the black dog waited. Its bristle-like fur was untouched by the rain, its red eyes watching me before it lifted its muzzle to the air and sniffed. The beast inhaled, scenting the city, the atmosphere crackling with electricity. I glanced quickly behind me, back toward the alley. It was silent but eerily still. Returning my attention to the dog, I wondered how close the demon was or if it was hunting me now? *Surely, I was no threat to this preternatural hound?* I felt a chill presence creeping from the alley behind me, but I remained still.

"Do I anger you, little poltergeist?" the demon asked from the shadows.

"Stay away from Nick," I said, turning slowly to face the demon that waited beyond the light.

It was formed entirely from shadow, wisps of darkness woven into a cloak, a cowl completely obscuring its face. Although I could not see its eyes, I felt the intensity of that malevolent gaze. I stiffened, pulling more energy into myself. I needed all my strength against this demon. It had weakened me during life, delighting at my fragility until I could fight it no longer. But I would not be so easily defeated again.

"Are you eager for battle now, little

poltergeist?" the demon mocked, moving toward me, shadows summoned from the surrounding street to pool darkly around its cloak.

"Leave Nick alone," I repeated, steeling myself for an attack as it toyed with me.

The thing laughed, throwing its head back to reveal a bone-white face. I stared at those perfect features; the symmetry so complete it was alarming. The demon smiled at me, showing its tiny white teeth, each perfect and squared like the teeth of a child, unnerving in an adult face. I shuddered in revulsion, backing away from the shadows that now writhed across the pavement with each step it took toward me.

A low growl rumbled through the

street, thunder echoing across the city. Above, lightning split the midnight sky, bright and brilliant, casting Nick into silhouette as he raised a hand against the glare. I stumbled further from the reaching shadows, hoping to lure the demon away from Nick, but again, thunder broke my concentration, flashes of lightning illuminating the streetscape in quick succession. Fortunately, Nick was already walking away, past the massive hound that now stalked toward me and the demon.

"You couldn't defeat me before," the demon said, head cocked in curiosity as I stood motionless. "You haven't the strength to resist me even now. Relinquish your rage and vengeance, Alisha. Then you may have peace."

"You promised me that once before," I hissed.

The hound had circled behind the demon and now stopped a few paces behind it, red eyes bright with excitement. It howled, a terrifying challenge. Lightning struck the nearby cathedral spire, sending a shuddering impact through the sky and ground. Partially blinded by the lightning strike, I only glimpsed the shocked expression on the demon's twisted features before it turned, shadows swirling about it in a mass of darkness, and disappeared. I blinked in surprise, successive lightning strikes blinding me further, but the hound wasted no time, baying in a frenzied pursuit, thunder echoing over the city as the thunderstorm rolled toward the Southern

Ocean.

I stared at the empty space where the demon and the hound had been. Cold terror clawed at me with the horrible, sinking suspicion that the demon knew Nick; intended him now as a final torment for me. More than ever, I needed to save Nick and to do it quickly—I needed help to ambush my prey.

I focused on the distant thunderstorm along the coastline and summoned the energy within myself. The force of my will enacted was like an explosion, the released energy rattling nearby glass windows in their frames and summoning a gale in my wake. Concentrating all my will on finding the hound, I neared the massive thunderstorm suspended over the sea, the cloud mass gathering along the Mornington Peninsula. When I had been a teen, I'd visited similar pleasant-looking beaches with headlands overlooking small coves facing the Southern Ocean. These popular holiday destinations were sinister tonight, a single grey-green funnel of swirling cloud stretching down to an isolated cove; lightning snaking across the horizon where sea met sky. A foreboding spread through the night and I knew I was closing in on my quarry.

I slipped unobtrusively through the maelstrom below me, my form coalescing on the shore of a small, deserted cove. Another menacing rumble of thunder shook the night, and I glanced at the ocean, waters of this small bay marked by wild white-capped waves, the steep cliffs to my right, in front and behind me pounded by the swell. Directly before me, narrow ruins of a pier stood resolute against the waves. If the demon was here to feed, it needed a victim. Looking more closely at the old pier, I noticed the remnants of planks tied to the supports, buttressed against the sandstone cliff. Behind the pier, there would probably be a cave or hollow in the cliff where those desperate for shelter might choose to hide.

I drew closer to the little pier, aware of a pervasive hush across the landscape, dulling the roar of the ocean and the storm. The demon was close, I could feel its malignant presence. A low growl rumbled through the storm, energy quickening through the cove, and beneath it, scarcely audible, a whimpering sigh from within the hollow cliff face. Silence fell over the cove. In taking a life, had the demon somehow stopped the world around me? I waited, the surrounding silence claustrophobic.

Suddenly, it shattered. Fierce baying of the pursuing hound was joined by the deafening slap of waves against the shore, and the roar of the wind against the craggy headland. The demon emerged from the sandstone hollow, a cloak of shadows billowing in the gale. It moved with an almost lazy, satisfied manner that repulsed me, its symmetrical face more frightening than if it were scarred and horned. I screamed my outrage, but the demon turned and smiled, white teeth a parody of welcome before it vanished from the beach in a swirl of dark shadows.

The sound and power of the thunderstorm erupted around me. Sand hissed past me as the waves from the small bay suddenly hurled themselves against the cliffs. Lightning forked across the clouds, illuminating the sky, and revealing momentarily, the huge black dog on the rocky headland above me. A bolt of lightning hit a dead tree in the sand dunes, and I jerked with surprise. I tried to calm myself, think clearly.

I felt the presence of the hound was behind me on the beach before I heard it. Carefully I turned around, the muscles of those massive shoulders bunching powerfully as it stalked toward me. I did not meet the red eyes but was uncomfortably aware of its gaze never leaving me. I remained still, hoping I presented no threat to such a predatory supernatural beast. But the hound snarled, lips lifting to reveal long, white fangs which, like those of the demon, were unnaturally white. I shivered with an inexplicable understanding that these predators did not tear flesh and but instead, their teeth were stained with the spirit they feasted upon.

"Let me join you," I said quietly to the hound, but its hackles lifted as I spoke.

I steadied myself, calming my fear as the dog circled me again, a low snarl rumbling through its chest and reverberating through the storm above me.

I did not move as it inhaled my scent, its large paws leaving no tracks on the sand.

"Let me join your hunt," I said again as the dog completed its second circle. "Your quarry and mine are the same. Let us hunt together."

The hound watched me with those intelligent eyes, somehow conveying what a foolish idiot I was. I nodded in silent acknowledgment, realised to a hunter like the hound, I had little to possibly offer.

"I can help corner your quarry as I did earlier this evening," I offered. "Then it is yours. Will you not let me join in your hunt?"

Those uncanny red eyes fixed on me, tension growing taunt around us as the hound considered my words. The tempest stilled and very slowly, the red eyes slid from mine and the hound gave an audible snort, before turning and trotting away, not waiting to see if I followed. Around me, the thunderstorm roared back to life as the hound howled again, the thrill of the hunt echoing into the storm. Wearily, I summoned the reserves of my energy and followed.

The hound tracked our quarry to a densely populated area of Melbourne I knew well. I stood outside a very familiar house; an ordinary two-storey terrace Nick had inherited from his grandmother. I had expected to see the tidy paved courtyard and neatly trimmed trees that led to the front wide porch. Instead, I stared with the black dog beside me at what might have been a stranger's house. The porch was no longer meticulously swept, old newspapers had piled in one corner and the hedges were overgrown. Fear uncurled in me like a live creature and I laid a trembling hand on the broad shoulders of the hound. Quickly, I jerked my hand away, startled by my own careless gesture, but the hound had not resisted. Instead, it turned its massive head upward to regard me with an expression of concern.

"Let me go in first," I said. "When the demon is distracted, it doesn't notice you."

The intelligent eyes brightened at my plan, and the muzzle lifted skyward, scenting the approaching dawn. In silent agreement, its focus returned to the front door, and I exhaled slowly, expelling my energy as the wrought-iron gate clanged open and I moved toward the house.

The front door was unlocked, offering no resistance as it burst open, bouncing off the opposing wall. This had been my house too when Nick had invited me to live here with him. Ignoring the dark hallway, dusty curtains drawn across the bay-widows and unopened mail piled on the kitchen bench, I headed straight for the small sitting room at the side of the house where I knew Nick would be. I hurried past the spiderwebs, stirring dust and a few leaves on the floor with my passage. Nick was fastidiously tidy and to see his home so despondent made me furious. My resolution only grew to rip the demon from him and the harm it had inflicted.

Nick's voice called from the back room, so faint I'd almost missed it amid the chaotic noise of my entrance. I hesitated, considering if this was a strategy by the demon to lure me into another trap. But I decided I didn't care. I needed to save Nick now or I would lose him. Still, I did not blindly rampage into the back room, but entered cautiously into the dimly lit space, hardly a whisper of sound accompanying my movement.

Curtains drawn across the main windows meant the only light came from the tall side-windows opening onto a paved courtyard and koi-pond. I glanced through these net curtains at the courtyard beyond, wrinkling my face at the filthy koi-pond. I looked to the sofa along the far wall where

Nick lay motionless, frowning at dust motes swirling frantically in the light. His eyes flickered toward me with vague awareness, but then he half-closed them again.

"Alisha," the demon greeted me instead.

I turned my gaze to the darkness behind the sofa, and the demon emerging from its shadow camouflage. It smiled that wretched parody again, an oily darkness spreading across the far wall behind it. I moved directly in front of Nick, noticing how emaciated he was without the overcoat to hide it. His eyes were dull with pain and desperation. I remembered those final moments too well. I imagined I had looked like that too before the end.

"You know he doesn't have long, don't you, Alisha?" the demon asked, stepping toward me.

Nick's eyelids fluttered weakly, and I knew he couldn't see me, but somehow, he seemed aware of me. The demon's words were directed at me, but enough of the intelligent man I loved remained for those same words to provoke him to question everything. This was the Nick I had loved. This was the man I knew could save himself, but he needed my help first.

"I asked you to leave him alone," I told the demon, my gaze never leaving Nick.

Thunder rolled across the sky, and outside the house, the hound howled its frustration. The demon jerked as if struck, and I knew I needed to act now.

Summoning all the anger, rage, hopelessness, and pain of my death, I added the love, kindness, strength, and hope Nick had shown me during my life, and poured it into a single word.

"Nick!" I screamed.

His name reverberated through the dusty house, rattling doors and tumbling books onto the floor. The demon hissed in outrage, shadows roiling toward me like a living mass. But I was a strength now that would not be denied. I stood resolute before Nick and made him *see* me. His eyes widened in shock and he reached for me.

"Alisha?" he asked with wonder.

"Don't listen to that *thing*," I told him, pointing at the demon as though I could strike it to ashes.

"Nick," it began, a wide smile revealing white teeth, pale skin stretching grotesquely.

"Liar!" I warned, voice quavering with the effort to sustain this physical presence. "Its words are a poisonous sorrow. It drained what hope I had, stole our future when it lied to me. Reject it please, Nick."

My plea spoken; what strength I had finally guttered then failed. I saw Nick's eyes searching the room for me, his concern escalating to fear.

"Alisha?" he called, voice shaking as he staggered to his feet.

"She's gone," the demon said with feigned disappointment. "Ghosts can't sustain themselves for long."

Nick turned, face impassive as he

stared, finally seeing the demon and not its silken promises. "Was what she said a lie?" he asked.

The demon narrowed its gaze. The shroud of falsehood woven tightly around Nick began to waver beneath his scrutiny. I watched Nick consider my words, carefully chosen from his own specialised knowledge, hoping he would understand their true meaning. He straightened and nodded grimly before staring coldly at the demon.

"Names have power over your kind, Acedia," he said, advancing on the demon as he named it.

I watched from my position outside of this battle, noticing each time Nick repeated the name, it struck like a blow, the demon's resolve weakening against Nick's power over it.

"Acedia," Nick finally shouted. "Demon of sorrow!"

The shadows coiled protectively about the demon. It retreated toward the window, still facing Nick, its face contorted in rage as he shouted its name again.

Suddenly, a tremor shook the earth. Nick and the demon were so focused on each other and the battle for dominance between them, that neither had noticed the trembling earth. Another tremor shook the floorboards and Acedia hissed, whipping the shadows about it as the window exploded inward, shards of glass thrown across the room.

The hound leapt through the shattered

window, barrelling Nick aside as it howled triumphantly, jaws snapping at wisps of shadow. I hurried forward to Nick, my hands hovering uselessly over his broken and cut body. Looking up in panic, I saw Acedia wrestle itself free and moving through the broken window in a flutter of shadows. Growling, the hound moved to follow but slid to a sudden halt in the paved courtyard beyond, its red eyes fixed on me.

"This is your hunt!" I shouted.

In answer, the hound bayed with appreciation, head thrown back to the storm, the sound electrifying the atmosphere as lightning flickered across the dawn sky. Without another glance to me, the dog leaped into the air and vanished into the roiling funnel of cloud rolling westward with the storm.

"Alisha," Nick murmured from the floor beside me.

I wanted to throw my arms around him, pull him tight to me and be held within his embrace. But Nick could no longer truly see me. I lifted my hand to touch him, but he didn't react. I thought maybe it was better that Nick could no longer perceive me. I was part of his past now, and the deep wounds Acedia had inflicted could never heal if he kept clinging to them.

Instead, I watched the thunderstorm continue west, imaging the battle within those clouds. I was apart from time and place now, the world around me like a dreamscape I would never wake from; the threads securing me to the tapestry of this world had been cut. The only anchor holding me firm now was the next thunderstorm, wondering if this time, I would answer that howling summons to join the hunt.

HER WATCHERS

By Laurence Sullivan

They had always been there…the three of them. Whenever there was bad news to bring, they'd appear unannounced. She had first seen them aged four, when Princess— her beloved pet gerbil—died. About an hour before little Princess fell victim to the Reaper, they were there. Three figures shrouded in cloaks with only their sunken eyes visible, just gazing listlessly at the little girl—Linda.

You would have thought that would strike fear into any little girl's heart, but no. She found them strangely comforting. As she grew older, she noticed the pattern of their appearance and even grew grateful to them—it gave her about an hour to work out who might be leaving the world and the time to be with them. Often that wasn't possible, but sometimes it was the ultimate blessing.

When her father had been in a coma, her cloaked harbingers bought her enough time to be with him in his final moments.

Linda's two sisters were grateful, too, though she never did explain to them exactly how she knew—they put it down to her being the favourite, and youngest daughter's intuition.

Today was different; she'd seen them while doing her washing. Staring at her through the window, warning her wordlessly of someone's impending doom.

Her mobile started ringing.

"Linda? It's Jill... Lucie, it's about Lucie. Don't be frightened, darling, but... Just get to the Shore Hospital as soon as you can, okay? No, no... Well, yes, it is serious; they think she may have had a stroke. Please, Linda, just get here as quickly as you can. I love you."

The call was abruptly ended.

Linda raced to grab her keys and practically leapt into her car, quickly catching sight of her loyal messengers in the interior mirror. With the ignition started, she drove as quickly as she could, running red lights wherever possible. The hospital was almost an hour away, going at a legal speed, but if she sped all the way she could do it in fifty minutes and be with her sister for those last precious moments.

Just as she was mere minutes away from her destination, her phone started ringing. As she looked down to answer it—tears mystifying her eyes—she swerved and crashed full force into an oncoming vehicle.

In her haste, she never thought to put her seatbelt on.

A click, then the sound of her own voice: "You've reached Linda, but sorry I can't get to the phone. Please leave your message and I'll get right back!"

"Linda, it's Jill. I've great news, darling—she's going to be all right! The doctors say she's going to be okay! It was a misdiagnosis—the tests came back clear. She'll be in here for a while, but there's no reason to rush now, so drive safe, please?"

Her sister's voice continued to fill Linda's ears as her world grew ever-darker—enveloping and soothing her like a blanket—as she unwillingly moved on to whatever world came next…

First published in Darker Times Fiction, 2013

THE HOWLING CASTLE

By Zoey Xolton

Mournful howls echoed through the old stone halls of the derelict castle, long abandoned to the moors. Carried by the wind, the unsettling sound flowed down dark stairwells, before dissipating into the vacuum of the great vaulted ceilings.

The castle was said to be haunted, but locals knew better. It was not earth-bound spirits that wailed, lost in time. *The Howling Castle* it was called, for it lived, breathed, and fed; an entity in its own right.

It cried out, tempting tourists to explore its decaying splendour…only to devour them body and soul, leaving no evidence of its macabre secret.

ABOUT THE PUBLISHER

BLACK HARE PRESS is a small, independent publisher based in Melbourne, Australia.

Founded in 2018, our aim has always been to champion emerging authors from all around the globe and offer opportunities for them to participate in speculative fiction and horror short story anthologies.

Connect

Website: *www.blackharepress.com*

Twitter: *@BlackHarePress*